Hadji Murad

Leo Tolstoy

Leo Tolstoy

Filiquarian Publishing, LLC is publishing this edition of Hadji Murad, due to its public domain status.

The cover design of Hadji Murad is copyright 2007, Filiquarian Publishing, LLC.

Filiquarian Publishing, LLC

Contents

Hadji Murad

Chapter I

I was returning home by the fields. It was midsummer, the hay
harvest was over and they were just beginning to reap the rye.
At that season of the year there is a delightful variety of
flowers — red, white, and pink scented tufty clover; milk-
white ox-eye daisies with their bright yellow centers and
pleasant spicy smell; yellow honey-scented rape blossoms; tall
campanulas with white and lilac bells, tulip-shaped; creeping
vetch; yellow, red, and pink scabious; faintly scented, neatly
arranged purple plaintains with blossoms slightly tinged with
pink; cornflowers, the newly opened blossoms bright blue in
the sunshine but growing paler and redder towards evening or
when growing old; and delicate almond-scented dodder flowers
that withered quickly. I gathered myself a large nosegay and
was going home when I noticed in a ditch, in full bloom, a
beautiful thistle plant of the crimson variety, which in our
neighborhood they call "Tartar" and carefully avoid when
mowing — or, if they do happen to cut it down, throw out from
among the grass for fear of pricking their hands. Thinking to
pick this thistle and put it in the center of my nosegay, I
climbed down into the ditch, and after driving away a velvety
bumble-bee that had penetrated deep into one of the flowers

and had there fallen sweetly asleep, I set to work to pluck the flower. But this proved a very difficult task. Not only did the stalk prick on every side — even through the handkerchief I wrapped round my hand — but it was so tough that I had to struggle with it for nearly five minutes, breaking the fibers one by one; and when I had at last plucked it, the stalk was all frayed and the flower itself no longer seemed so fresh and beautiful. Moreover, owing to a coarseness and stiffness, it did not seem in place among the delicate blossoms of my nosegay. I threw it away feeling sorry to have vainly destroyed a flower that looked beautiful in its proper place.

"But what energy and tenacity! With what determination it defended itself, and how dearly it sold its life!" thought I, remembering the effort it had cost me to pluck the flower. The way home led across black-earth fields that had just been ploughed up. I ascended the dusty path. The ploughed field belonged to a landed proprietor and was so large that on both sides and before me to the top of the hill nothing was visible but evenly furrowed and moist earth. The land was well tilled and nowhere was there a blade of grass or any kind of plant to be seen, it was all black. "Ah, what a destructive creature is man. . . . How many different plant-lives he destroys to support his own existence!" thought I, involuntarily looking around for some living thing in this lifeless black field. In front of me to the right of the road I saw some kind of little clump, and drawing nearer I found it was the same kind of thistle as that which I had vainly plucked and thrown away. This "Tartar" plant had three branches. One was broken and stuck out like the stump of a mutilated arm. Each of the other two bore a flower, once red but now blackened. One stalk was broken, and half of it hung down with a soiled flower at its tip. The other, though also soiled with black mud, still stood erect. Evidently a

6

cartwheel had passed over the plant but it had risen again, and that was why, though erect, it stood twisted to one side, as if a piece of its body had been torn from it, its bowels drawn out, an arm torn off, and one of its eyes plucked out. Yet it stood firm and did not surrender to man who had destroyed all its brothers around it. . . .

"What vitality!" I thought. "Man has conquered everything and destroyed millions of plants, yet this one won't submit." And I remembered a Caucasian episode of years ago, which I had partly seen myself, partly heard of from eye-witnesses, and in part imagined.

The episode, as it has taken shape in my memory and imagination, was as follows.

* * *

It happened towards the end of 1851.

On a cold November evening Hadji Murad rode into Makhmet, a hostile Chechen aoul that lay some fifteen miles from Russian territory and was filled with the scented smoke of burning Kizyak. The strained chant of the muezzin had just ceased, and though the clear mountain air, impregnated with kizyak smoke, above the lowing of the cattle and the bleating of the sheep that were dispersing among the saklyas (which were crowded together like the cells of honeycomb), could be clearly heard the guttural voices of disputing men, and sounds of women's and children's voices rising from near the fountain below.

7

This Hadji Murad was Shamil's naib, famous for his exploits, who used never to ride out without his banner and some dozens of murids, who caracoled and showed off before him. Now wrapped in a hood and burka, from under which protruded a rifle, he rode, a fugitive with one murid only, trying to attract as little attention as possible and peering with his quick black eyes into the faces of those he met on his way.

When he entered the aoul, instead of riding up the road leading to the open square, he turned to the left into a narrow side street, and on reaching the second saklya, which was cut into the hill side, he stopped and looked round. There was no one under the penthouse in front, but on the roof of the saklya itself, behind the freshly plastered clay chimney, lay a man covered with a sheepskin. Hadji Murad touched him with the handle of his leather-plaited whip and clicked his tongue, and an old man, wearing a greasy old beshmet and a nightcap, rose from under the sheepskin. His moist red eyelids had no lashes, and he blinked to get them unstuck. Hadji Murad, repeating the customary "Selaam aleikum!" uncovered his face. "aleikum, selaam!" said the old man, recognizing him, and smiling with his toothless mouth. And raising himself on his thin legs he began thrusting his feet into the wooden-heeled slippers that stood by the chimney. Then he leisurely slipped his arms into the sleeves of his crumpled sheepskin, and going to the ladder that leant against the roof he descended backwards, while he dressed and as he climbed down he kept shaking his head on its thin, shrivelled sunburnt neck and mumbling something with his toothless mouth. As soon as he reached the ground he hospitably seized Hadji Murad's bridle and right stirrup; but the strong active murid had quickly dismounted and motioning the old man aside, took his place. Hadji Murad also dismounted, and walking with a slight limp, entered under the penthouse. A boy of fifteen, coming quickly out of the door, met him and wonderingly fixed his sparkling eyes, black as ripe sloes, on the new arrivals.

"Run to the mosque and call your father," ordered the old man as he hurried forward to open the thin, creaking door into the saklya.

As Hadji Murad entered the outer door, a slight, spare, middle-aged woman in a yellow smock, red beshmet, and wide blue trousers came through an inner door carrying cushions.

"May thy coming bring happiness!" said she, and bending nearly double began arranging the cushions along the front wall for the guest to sit on.

"May thy sons live!" answered Hadji Murad, taking off his burka, his rifle, and his sword, and handing them to the old man who carefully hung the rifle and sword on a nail beside the weapons of the master of the house, which were suspended between two large basins that glittered against the clean clay-plastered and carefully whitewashed wall.

Hadji Murad adjusted the pistol at his back, came up to the cushions, and wrapping his Circassian coat closer round him, sat down. The old man squatted on his bare heels beside him, closed his eyes, and lifted his hands palms upwards. Hadji Murad did the same; then after repeating a prayer they both stroked their faces, passing their hands downwards till the palms joined at the end of their beards.

"Ne habar?" ("Is there anything new?") asked Hadji Murad, addressing the old man.

"Habar yok" ("Nothing new"), replied the old man, looking with his lifeless red eyes not at Hadji Murad's face but at his breast. "I live at the apiary and have only today come to see my son. . . . He knows."

Hadji Murad, understanding that the old man did not wish to say what he knew and what Hadji Murad wanted to know, slightly nodded his head and asked no more questions.

"There is no good news," said the old man. "The only news is that the hares keep discussing how to drive away the eagles, and the eagles tear first one and then another of them. The other day the Russian dogs burnt the hay in the Mitchit aoul. . . . May their faces be torn!" he added hoarsely and angrily.

Hadji Murad's murid entered the room, his strong legs striding softly over the earthen floor. Retaining only his dagger and pistol, he took off his burka, rifle, and sword as Hadji Murad had done, and hung them up on the same nails as his leader's weapons.

"Who is he?" asked the old man, pointing to the newcomer.

"My murid. Eldar is his name," said Hadji Murad.

"That is well," said the old man, and motioned Eldar to a place on a piece of felt beside Hadji Murad. Eldar sat down, crossing his legs and fixing his fine ram-like eyes on the old man who, having now started talking, was telling how their brave fellows had caught two Russian soldiers the week before and had killed one and sent the other to Shamil in Veden.

Hadji Murad

Hadji Murad heard him absently, looking at the door and listening to the sounds outside. Under the penthouse steps were heard, the door creaked, and Sado, the master of the house, came in. He was a man of about forty, with a small beard, long nose, and eyes as black, though not as glittering, as those of his fifteen-year-old son who had run to call him home and who now entered with his father and sat down by the door. The master of the house took off his wooden slippers at the door, and pushing his old and much-worn cap to the back of his head (which had remained unshaved so long that it was beginning to be overgrown with black hair), at once squatted down in front of Hadji Murad.

He too lifted his palms upwards, as the old man had done, repeated a prayer, and then stroked his face downwards. Only after that did he begin to speak. He told how an order had come from Shamil to seize Hadji Murad alive or dead, that Shamil's envoys had left only the day before, that the people were afraid to disobey Shamil's orders, and that therefore it was necessary to be careful.

"In my house," said Sado, "no one shall injure my kunak while I live, but how will it be in the open fields? . . . We must think it over."

Hadji Murad listened with attention and nodded approvingly. When Sado had finished he said:

"Very well. Now we must send a man with a letter to the Russians. My murid will go but he will need a guide."

"I will send brother Bata," said Sado. "Go and call Bata," he added, turning to his son.

The boy instantly bounded to his nimble feet as if he were on springs, and swinging his arms, rapidly left the saklya. Some ten minutes later he returned with a sinewy, short-legged Chechen, burnt almost black by the sun, wearing a worn and tattered yellow Circassian coat with frayed sleeves, and crumpled black leggings.

Hadji Murad greeted the newcomer, and again without wasting a single word, immediately asked:

"Canst thou conduct my murid to the Russians?"

"I can," gaily replied Bata. "I can certainly do it. There is not another Chechen who would pass as I can. Another might agree to go and might promise anything, but would do nothing; but I can do it!"

"All right," said Hadji Murad. "Thou shalt receive three for thy trouble," and he held up three fingers.

Bata nodded to show that he understood, and added that it was not money he prized, but that he was ready to serve Hadji Murad for the honor alone. Every one in the mountains knew Hadji Murad, and how he slew the Russian swine.

"Very well. . . . A rope should be long but a speech short," said Hadji Murad.

"Well then I'll hold my tongue," said Bata.

"Where the river Argun bends by the cliff," said Hadji Murad, "there are two stacks in a glade in the forest — thou knowest?"

"I know."

"There my four horsemen are waiting for me," said Hadji Murad.

"Aye," answered Bata, nodding.

"Ask for Khan Mahoma. He knows what to do and what to say. Canst thou lead him to the Russian Commander, Prince Vorontsov?"

"Yes, I'll take him."

"Canst thou take him and bring him back again?"

"I can."

"Then take him there and return to the wood. I shall be there too."

"I will do it all," said Bata, rising, and putting his hands on his heart he went out.

Hadji Murad turned to his host.

"A man must also be sent to Chekhi," he began, and took hold of one of the cartridge pouches of his Circassian coat, but let his hand drop immediately and became silent on seeing two women enter the saklya.

One was Sado's wife — the thin middle-aged woman who had arranged the cushions. The other was quite a young girl,

13

wearing red trousers and a green beshmet. A necklace of silver coins covered the whole front of her dress, and at the end of the short but thick plait of hard black hair that hung between her thin shoulder-blades a silver ruble was suspended. Her eyes, as sloe-black as those of her father and brother, sparkled brightly in her young face which tried to be stern. She did not look at the visitors, but evidently felt their presence.

Sado's wife brought in a low round table on which stood tea, pancakes in butter, cheese, churek (that is, thinly rolled out bread), and honey. The girl carried a basin, a ewer, and a towel.

Sado and Hadji Murad kept silent as long as the women, with their coin ornaments tinkling, moved softly about in their red soft-soled slippers, setting out before the visitors the things they had brought. Eldar sat motionless as a statue, his ram-like eyes fixed on his crossed legs, all the time the women were in the saklya. Only after they had gone and their soft footsteps could no longer be heard behind the door, did he give a sigh of relief.

Hadji Murad having pulled out a bullet from one of the cartridge-pouches of his Circassian coat, and having taken out a rolled-up note that lay beneath it, held it out, saying:

"To be handed to my son."

"Where must the answer be sent?"

"To thee; and thou must forward it to me."

"It shall be done," said Sado, and placed the note in the cartridge-pocket of his own coat. Then he took up the metal ewer and moved the basin towards Hadji Murad.

Hadji Murad turned up the sleeves of his beshmet on his white muscular arms, held out his hands under the clear cold water which Sado poured from the ewer, and having wiped them on a clean unbleached towel, turned to the table. Eldar did the same. While the visitors ate, Sado sat opposite and thanked them several times for their visit. The boy sat by the door never taking his sparkling eyes off Hadji Murad's face, and smiled as if in confirmation of his father's words.

Though he had eaten nothing for more than twenty-four hours Hadji Murad ate only a little bread and cheese; then, drawing out a small knife from under his dagger, he spread some honey on a piece of bread.

"Our honey is good," said the old man, evidently pleased to see Hadji Murad eating his honey. "This year, above all other years, it is plentiful and good."

"I thank thee," said Hadji Murad and turned from the table. Eldar would have liked to go on eating but he followed his leader's example, and having moved away from the table, handed him the ewer and basin.

Sado knew that he was risking his life by receiving such a guest in his house, for after his quarrel with Shamil the latter had issued a proclamation to all the inhabitants of Chechnya forbidding them to receive Hadji Murad on pain of death. He knew that the inhabitants of the aoul might at any moment become aware of Hadji Murad's presence in his house and might demand his surrender. But this not only did not frighten Sado, it even gave him pleasure with himself because he was doing his duty.

"Whilst thou are in my house and my head is on my shoulders no one shall harm thee," he repeated to Hadji Murad.

Hadji Murad looked into his glittering eyes and understanding that this was true, said with some solemnity —

"Mayst thou receive joy and life!"

Sado silently laid his hand on his heart in token of thanks for these kind words.

Having closed the shutters of the saklya and laid some sticks in the fireplace, Sado, in an exceptionally bright and animated mood, left the room and went into that part of his saklya where his family all lived. The women had not yet gone to sleep, and were talking about the dangerous visitors who were spending the night in their guest chambers.

Chapter II

At Vozvizhensk, the advanced fort situated some ten miles from the aoul in which Hadji Murad was spending the night, three soldiers and a non-commissioned officer left the fort and went beyond the Shahgirinsk Gate. The soldiers, dressed as Caucasian soldiers used to be in those days, wore sheepskin coats and caps, and boots that reached above their knees, and they carried their cloaks tightly rolled up and fastened across their shoulders. Shouldering arms, they first went some five hundred paces along the road and then turned off it and went some twenty paces to the right — the dead leaves rustling under their boots — till they reached the blackened trunk of a broken plane tree just visible through the darkness. There they stopped. It was at this plane tree that an ambush party was usually placed.

The bright stars, that had seemed to be running along the tree tops while the soldiers were walking through the forest, now stood still, shining brightly between the bare branches of the trees.

"A good job it's dry," said the non-commissioned officer Panov, bringing down his long gun and bayonet with a clang from his shoulder and placing it against the plane tree.

The three soldiers did the same.

"Sure enough I've lost it!" muttered Panov crossly. "Must have left it behind or I've dropped it on the way."

"What are you looking for?" asked one of the soldiers in a bright, cheerful voice.

"The bowl of my pipe. Where the devil has it got to?"

"Have you got the stem?" asked the cheerful voice.

"Here it is."

"Then why not stick it straight into the ground?"

"Not worth bothering!"

"We'll manage that in a minute."

Smoking in ambush was forbidden, but this ambush hardly deserved the name. It was rather an outpost to prevent the mountaineers from bringing up a cannon unobserved and firing at the fort as they used to. Panov did not consider it necessary to forego the pleasure of smoking, and therefore accepted the cheerful soldier's offer. the latter took a knife from his pocket and made a small round hole in the ground. Having smoothed it, he adjusted the pipe stem to it, then filled the hole with tobacco and pressed it down, and the pipe was ready. A sulphur match flared and for a moment lit up the broad-cheeked face of the soldier who lay on his stomach, the air whistled in the stem, and Panov smelt the pleasant odor of burning tobacco.

"Fixed ut up?" said he, rising to his feet.

"Why, of course!"

"What a smart chap you are, Avdeev! . . . As wise as a judge! Now then, lad."

Avdeev rolled over on his side to make room for Panov, letting smoke escape from his mouth.

Panov lay down prone, and after wiping the mouthpiece with his sleeve, began to inhale.

When they had had their smoke the soldiers began to talk.

"They say the commander has had his fingers in the cashbox again," remarked one of them in a lazy voice. "He lost at cards, you see."

"He'll pay it back again," said Panov.

"Of course he will! He's a good officer," assented Avdeev.

"Good! good!" gloomily repeated the man who had started the conversation. "In my opinion the company ought to speak to him. 'If you've taken the money, tell us how much and when you'll repay it.'"

"That will be as the company decides," said Panov, tearing himself away from the pipe.

"Of course. 'The community is a strong man,'" assented Avdeev, quoting a proverb.

"There will be oats to buy and boots to get towards spring. the money will be wanted, and what shall we do if he's pocketed it?" insisted the dissatisfied one.

"I tell you it will be as the company wishes," repeated Panov. "It's not the first time; he takes it and gives it back."

In the Caucasus in those days each company chose men to manage its own commissariat. they received 6 rubles 50 kopeks a month per man from the treasury, and catered for the company. They planted cabbages, made hay, had their own carts, and prided themselves on their well-fed horses. The company's money was kept in a chest of which the commander had the key, and it often happened that he borrowed from the chest. This had just happened again, and the soldiers were talking about it. The morose soldier, Nikitin, wished to demand an account from the commander, while Panov and Avdeev considered that unnecessary.

After Panov, Nikitin had a smoke, and then spreading his cloak on the ground sat down on it leaning against the trunk of the plane tree. The soldiers were silent. Far above their heads the crowns of the trees rustled in the wind and suddenly, above this incessant low rustling, rose the howling, whining, weeping and chuckling of jackals.

"Just listen to those accursed creatures — how they caterwaul!"

"They're laughing at you because your mouth's all on one side," remarked the high voice of the third soldier, an Ukrainian.

All was silent again, except for the wind that swayed the branches, now revealing and now hiding the stars.

"I say, Panov," suddenly asked the cheerful Avdeev, "do you ever feel dull?"

"Dull, why?" replied Panov reluctantly.

"Well, I do. . . . I feel so dull sometimes that I don't know what I might not be ready to do to myself."

"There now!" was all Panov replied.

"That time when I drank all the money it was from dullness. It took hold of me . . . took hold of me till I thought to myself, 'I'll just get blind drunk!'"

"But sometimes drinking makes it still worse."

"Yes, that's happened to me too. But what is a man to do with himself?"

"But what makes you feel so dull?"

"What, me? . . . Why, it's the longing for home."

"Is yours a wealthy home then?"

"No; we weren't wealthy, but things went properly — we lived well." And Avdeev began to relate what he had already told Panov many times.

"You see, I went as a soldier of my own free will, instead of my brother," he said. "He has children. They were five in family and I had only just married. Mother began begging me to go. So I thought, 'Well, maybe they will remember what I've done.' So I went to our proprietor . . . he was a good master and he said, 'You're a fine fellow, go!' So I went instead of my brother."

"Well, that was right," said Panov.

"And yet, will you believe me, Panov, it's chiefly because of that that I feel so dull now? 'Why did you go instead of your brother?' I say to myself. 'He's living like a king now over there, while you have to suffer here;' and the more I think of it the worse I feel. . . . It seems just a piece of ill-luck!"

Avdeev was silent.

"Perhaps we'd better have another smoke," said he after a pause.

"Well then, fix it up!"

But the soldiers were not to have their smoke. Hardly had Avdeev risen to fix the pipe stem in its place when above the rustling of the trees they heard footsteps along the road. Panov took his gun and pushed Nikitin with his foot.

Nikitin rose and picked up his cloak.

The third soldier, Bondarenko, rose also, and said:

"And I have dreamt such a dream, mates. . . ."

"Sh!" said Avdeev, and the soldiers held their breath, listening. The footsteps of men in soft-soled boots were heard approaching. The fallen leaves and dry twigs could be heard rustling clearer and clearer through the darkness. Then came the peculiar guttural tones of Chechen voices. The soldiers could now not only hear men approaching, but could see two shadows passing through a clear space between the trees; one shadow taller than the other. When these shadows had come in line with the soldiers, Panov, gun in hand, stepped out on to the road, followed by his comrades.

"Who goes there?" cried he.

"Me, friendly Chechen," said the shorter one. This was Bata. "Gun, yok! . . . sword, yok!" said he, pointing to himself. "Prince, want!"

The taller one stood silent beside his comrade. He too was unarmed.

"He means he's a scout, and wants the Colonel," explained Panov to his comrades.

"Prince Vorontsov . . . much want! Big business!" said Bata.

"All right, all right! We'll take you to him," said Panov. "I say, you'd better take them," said he to Avdeev, "you and Bondarenko; and when you've given them up to the officer on duty come back again. Mind," he added, "be careful to make them keep in front of you!"

"And what of this?" said Avdeev, moving his gun and bayonet as though stabbing someone. "I's just give a dig, and let the steam out of him!"

"What'll he be worth when you've stuck him?" remarked Bondarenko.

"Now, march!"

When the steps of the two soldiers conducting the scouts could no longer be heard, Panov and Nikitin returned to their post.

"What the devil brings them here at night?" said Nikitin.

"Seems it's necessary," said panov. "But it's getting chilly," he added, and unrolling his cloak he put it on and sat down by the tree.

About two hours later Avdeev and Bondarenko returned.

"Well, have you handed them over?"

"Yes. They weren't yet asleep at the Colonel's — they were taken straight in to him. And do you know, mates, those shaven-headed lads are fine!" continued Avdeev. "Yes, really. What a talk I had with them!"

"Of course you'd talk," remarked Nikitin disapprovingly.

"Really they're just like Russians. One of them is married. 'Molly,' says I, 'bar?' 'Bar,' he says. Bondarenko, didn't I say 'bar'? 'Many bar?' 'A couple,' says he. A couple! Such a good talk we had! Such nice fellows!"

"Nice, indeed!" said Nikitin. "If you met him alone he'd soon let the guts out of you."

"It will be getting light before long." said panov.

"Yes, the stars are beginning to go out," said Avdeev, sitting down and making himself comfortable.

And the soldiers were silent again.

Leo Tolstoy

Chapter III

The windows of the barracks and the soldiers' houses had long been dark in the fort; but there were still lights in the windows of the best house.

In it lived Prince Simon Mikhailovich Vorontsov, Commander of the Kurin Regiment, an Imperial Aide-de-Camp and son of the Commander-in-Chief. Vorontsov's wife, Marya Vasilevna, a famous Petersburg beauty, was with him and they lived in this little Caucasian fort more luxuriously than any one had ever lived there before. To Vorontsov, and even more to his wife, it seemed that they were not only living a very modest life, but one full of privations, while to the inhabitants of the place their luxury was surprising and extraordinary.

Just now, at midnight, the host and hostess sat playing cards with their visitors, at a card table lit by four candles, in the spacious drawing room with its carpeted floor and rich curtains drawn across the windows. Vorontsov, who had a long face and wore the insignia and gold cords of an aide-de-camp, was partnered by a shaggy young man of gloomy appearance, a graduate of Petersburg University whom Princess Vorontsov had lately had sent to the Caucasus to be tutor to her little son (born of her first marriage). Against them played two officers: one a broad, red-faced man, Poltoratsky, a company commander who had exchanged out of the Guards; and the other the regimental adjutant, who sat very straight on his chair with a cold expression on his handsome face.

Princess Marya Vasilevna, a large-built, large-eyed, black-browed beauty, sat beside Poltoratsky — her crinoline touching his lets — and looked over his cards. In her words, her looks, her smile, her perfume, and in every movement of her body, there was something that reduced Poltoratsky to obliviousness of everything except the consciousness of her nearness, and he made blunder after blunder, trying his partner's temper more and more.

"No . . . that's too bad! You've wasted an ace again," said the regimental adjutant, flushing all over as Poltoratsky threw out an ace.

Poltoratsky turned his kindly, wide-set black eyes towards the dissatisfied adjutant uncomprehendingly, as though just aroused from sleep.

"Do forgive him!" said Marya Vasilevna, smiling. "There, you see! Didn't I tell you so?" she went on, turning to Poltoratsky.

"But that's not at all what you said," replied Poltoratsky, smiling.

"Wasn't it?" she queried, with an answering smile, which excited and delighted Poltoratsky to such a degree that he blushed crimson and seeing the cards began to shuffle.

"It isn't your turn to deal," said the adjutant sternly, and with his white ringed hand he began to deal himself, as though he wished to get rid of the cards as quickly as possible.

The prince's valet entered the drawing room and announced that the officer on duty wanted to speak to him.

"Excuse me, gentlemen," said the prince speaking Russian with an English accent. "Will you take my place, marya?"

"Do you all agree?" asked the princess, rising quickly and lightly to her full height, rustling her silks, and smiling the radiant smile of a happy woman.

"I always agree to everything," replied the adjutant, very pleased that the princess — who could not play at all — was now going to play against him.

Poltoratsky only spread out his hands and smiled.

The rubber was nearly finished when the prince returned to the drawing room, animated and obviously very pleased.

"Do you know what I propose?"

"What?"

"That we have some champagne."

"I am always ready for that," said Poltoratsky.

"Why not? We shall be delighted!" said the adjutant.

"Bring some, Vasili!" said the prince.

"What did they want you for?" asked Marya Vasilevna.

"It was the officer on duty and another man."

"Who? What about?" asked Marya Vasilevna quickly.

"I mustn't say," said Vorontsov, shrugging his shoulders.

"You mustn't say!" repeated Marya Vasilevna. "We'll see about that."

When the champagne was brought each of the visitors drank a glass, and having finished the game and settled the scores they began to take their leave.

"Is it your company that's ordered to the forest tomorrow?" the prince asked Poltoratsky as they said goodbye.

"Yes, mine . . . why?"

"Then we shall meet tomorrow," said the prince, smiling slightly.

"Very pleased," replied Poltoratsky, not quite understanding what Vorontsov was saying to him and preoccupied only by the thought that he would in a minute be pressing Marya Vasilevna's hand.

Marya Vasilevna, according to her wont, not only pressed his hand firmly but shook it vigorously, and again reminding him of his mistake in playing diamonds, she gave him what he took to be a delightful, affectionate, and meaning smile.

Poltoratsky went home in an ecstatic condition only to be understood by people like himself who, having grown up and been educated in society, meet a woman belonging to their own circle after months of isolated military life, and moreover a woman like Princess Vorontsov.

When he reached the little house in which he and his comrade lived he pushed the door, but it was locked. He knocked, with no result. He felt vexed, and began kicking the door and banging it with his sword. Then he heard a sound of footsteps and Vovilo — a domestic serf of his — undid the cabin hook which fastened the door.

"What do you mean by locking yourself in, blockhead?"

"But how is it possible, sir . . . ?"

"You're tipsy again! I'll show you 'how it is possible!'" and Poltoratsky was about to strike Vovilo but changed his mind. "Oh, go to the devil! . . . Light a candle."

"In a minute."

Vovilo was really tipsy. He had been drinking at the name day party of the ordnance sergeant, Ivan Petrovich. On returning home he began comparing his life with that of the latter. Ivan Petrovich had a salary, was married, and hoped in a year's time to get his discharge.

Vovilo had been taken "up" when a boy — that is, he had been taken into his owner's household service — and now although he was already over forty he was not married, but lived a campaigning life with his harum-scarum young master. He was a good master, who seldom struck him, but what kind of a life was it? "He promised to free me when we return from the Caucasus, but where am I to with my freedom? . . . It's a dog's life!" thought Vovilo, and he felt so sleepy that, afraid lest someone should come in and steal something, he fastened the hook of the door and fell asleep.

* * *

Poltoratsky entered the bedroom which he shared with his comrade Tikhonov.

"Well, have you lost?" asked Tikhonov, waking up.

"No, as it happens, I haven't. I've won seventeen rubles, and we drank a bottle of Cliquot!"

"And you've looked at Marya Vasilevna?"

"Yes, and I have looked at Marya Vasilevna," repeated Poltoratsky.

"It will soon be time to get up," said Tikhonov. "We are to start at six."

"Vovilo!" shouted Poltoratsky, "see that you wake me up properly tomorrow at five!"

"How can I wake you if you fight?"

"I tell you you're to wake me! Do you hear?"

"All right." Vovilo went out, taking Poltoratsky's boots and clothes with him. Poltoratsky got into bed and smoked a cigarette and put out his candle smiling the while. In the dark he saw before him the smiling face of Marya Vasilevna.

* * *

The Vorontsovs did not go to bed at once. When the visitors had left, Marya Vasilevna went up to her husband and standing in front of him, said severely —

"Eh bien! vous allez me dire ce que c'est."

"Mais, ma chere . . ."

"Pas de 'ma chere'! C'etait un emissaire, n'est-ce pas?"

"Quand meme, je ne puis pas vous le dire."

"Vous ne pouvez pas? Alors, c'est moi qui vais vous le dire!"

"Vous?"

"It was Hadji Murad, wasn't it?" said Marya Vasilevna, who had for some days past heard of the negotiations and thought that Hadji Murad himself had been to see her husband. Vorontsov could not altogether deny this, but disappointed her by saying that it was not Hadji Murad himself but only an emissary to announce that Hadji Murad would come to meet him next day at the spot where a wood-cutting expedition had been arranged.

In the monotonous life of the fortress the young Vorontsovs — both husband and wife — were glad of this occurrence, and it was already past two o'clock when, after speaking of the pleasure the news would give his father, they went to bed.

Chapter IV

After the three sleepless nights he had passed flying from the murids Shamil had sent to capture him, Hadji Murad fell asleep as soon as Sado, having bid him goodnight, had gone out of the saklya. He slept fully dressed with his head on his hand, his elbow sinking deep into the red down-cushions his host had arranged for him.

At a little distance, by the wall, slept Eldar. He lay on his back, his strong young limbs stretched out so that his high chest, with the black cartridge-pouches sewn into the front of his white Circassian coat, was higher than his freshly shaven, blue-gleaming head, which had rolled off the pillow and was thrown back. His upper lip, on which a little soft down was just appearing, pouted like a child's, now contracting and now expanding, as though he were sipping something. Like Hadji Murad he slept with pistol and dagger in his belt. the sticks in the grate burnt low, and a night light in a niche in the wall gleamed faintly.

In the middle of the night the floor of the guest-chamber creaked, and Hadji Murad immediately rose, putting his hand to his pistol. Sado entered, treading softly on the earthen floor.

"What is it?" asked Hadji Murad, as if he had not been asleep at all.

"We must think," replied Sado, squatting down in front of him. "A woman from her roof saw you arrive and told her husband, and now the whole aoul knows. A neighbor has just been to tell my wife that the Elders have assembled in the mosque and want to detain you."

"I must be off!" said Hadji Murad.

"The horses are saddled," said Sado, quickly leaving the saklya.

"Eldar!" whispered Hadji Murad. And Eldar, hearing his name, and above all his master's voice, leapt to his feet, setting his cap straight as he did so.

Hadji Murad put on his weapons and then his burka. Eldar did the same, and they both went silently out of the saklya into the penthouse. The black-eyed boy brought their horses. Hearing the clatter of hoofs on the hard-beaten road, someone stuck his head out of the door of a neighboring saklya and a man ran up the hill towards the mosque, clattering with his wooden shoes. There was no moon, but the stars shone brightly in the black sky so that the outlines of the saklya roofs could be seen in the darkness, the mosque with its minarets in the upper part of the village rising above the other buildings. From the mosque came a hum of voices.

Hadji Murad

Quickly seizing his gun, Hadji Murad placed his foot in the narrow stirrup, and silently and easily throwing his body across, swung himself onto the high cushion of the saddle.

"May God reward you!" he said, addressing his host while his right foot felt instinctively for the stirrup, and with his whip he lightly touched the lad who held his horse, as a sign that he should let go. The boy stepped aside, and the horse, as if it knew what it had to do, started at a brisk pace down the lane towards the principal street. Eldar rode behind him. Sado in his sheepskin followed, almost running, swinging his arms and crossing now to one side and now to the other of the narrow sidestreet. At the place where the streets met, first one moving shadow and then another appeared in the road.

"Stop . . . who's that? Stop!" shouted a voice, and several men blocked the path.

Instead of stopping, Hadji Murad drew his pistol from his belt and increasing his speed rode straight at those who blocked the way. They separated, and without looking round he started down the road at a swift canter. Eldar followed him at a sharp trot. Two shots cracked behind them and two bullets whistled past without hitting either Hadji Murad or Eldar. Hadji Murad continued riding at the same pace, but having gone some three hundred yards he stopped his slightly panting horse and listened.

In front of him, lower down, gurgled rapidly running water. Behind him in the aoul cocks crowed, answering one another. Above these sounds he heard behind him the approaching tramp of horses and the voices of several men. Hadji Murad touched his horse and rode on at an even pace. Those behind him galloped and soon overtook him. They were some twenty mounted men, inhabitants of the aoul, who had decided to detain Hadji Murad or a least to make a show of detaining him in order to justify themselves in Shamil's eyes. When they came near enough to be seen in the darkness, Hadji Murad stopped, let go his bridle, and with an accustomed movement of his bridle, and with an accustomed movement of his left hand unbuttoned the cover of his rifle, which he drew forth with his right. Eldar did the same.

"What do you want?" cried Hadji Murad. "Do you wish to take me? . . . Take me, then!" and he raised his rifle. The men form the aoul stopped, and Hadji Murad, rifle in hand, rode down into the ravine. the mounted men followed him but did not draw any nearer. When Hadji Murad had crossed to the other side of the ravine the men shouted to him that he should hear what they had to say. In reply he fired his rifle and put his horse to a gallop. When he reined it in his pursuers were no longer within hearing and the crowing of the cocks could also no longer be heard; only the murmur of the water in the forest sounded more distinctly and now and then came the cry of an owl. The black wall of the forest appeared quite close. It was in the forest that his murids awaited him.

On reaching it Hadji Murad paused, and drawing much air into his lungs he whistled and then listened silently. the next minute he was answered by a similar whistle from the forest. Hadji Murad turned from the road and entered it. When he had gone about a hundred paces he saw among the trunks of the trees a bonfire, the shadows of some men sitting round it, and, half lit-up by the firelight, a hobbled horse which was saddled. Four men were sitting by the fire.

Hadji Murad

One of them rose quickly, and coming up to Hadji Murad took hold of his bridle and stirrup. This was Hadji Murad's sworn brother who managed his household affairs for him.

"Put out the fire," said Hadji Murad, dismounting.

The men began scattering the pile and trampling on the burning branches.

"Has Bata been here?" asked Hadji Murad, moving towards a burka that was spread on the ground.

"Yes, he went away long ago with Khan Mahoma."

"Which way did they go?"

"That way," answered Khanefi pointing in the opposite direction to that from which Hadji Murad had come.

"All right," said Hadji Murad, and unslinging his rifle he began to load it.

"We must take care — I have been pursued," he said to a man who was putting out the fire.

This was Gamzalo, a Chechen. Gamzalo approached the barka, took up a rifle that lay on it wrapped in its cover, and without a word went to that side of the glade from which Hadji Murad had come.

When Eldar had dismounted he took Hadji Murad's horse, and having reined up both horses's heads high, tied them to two trees. Then he shouldered his rifle as Gamzalo had done and went to the other side of the glade. The bonfire was extinguished, the forest no longer looked as black as before, but in the sky the stars still shone, thought faintly.

Lifting his eyes to the stars and seeing that the Pleiades had already risen half-way up in the sky, Hadji Murad calculated that it must be long past midnight and that his nightly prayer was long overdue. He asked Khanefi for a ewer (they always carried one in their packs), and putting on his barka went to the water.

Having taken off his shoes and performed his ablutions, Hadji Murad stepped onto the burka with bare feet and then squatted down on his calves, and having first placed his fingers in his ears and closed his eyes, he turned to the south and recited the usual prayer.

When he had finished he returned to the place where the saddle bags lay, and sitting down on the burka he leant his elbows on his knees and bowed his head and fell into deep thought.

Hadji Murad always had great faith in his own fortune. When planning anything he always felt in advance firmly convinced of success, and fate smiled on him. It had been so, with a few rare exceptions, during the whole course of his stormy militray life; and so he hoped it would be now. He pictured to himself how — with the army Vorontsov would place at his disposal — he would march against Shamil and take him prisoner, and revenge himself on him; and how the russian Tsar would reward him and how he would again rule not only over Avaria, but over the whole of Chechnya, which would submit to him. With these thoughts he unwittingly fell asleep.

Hadji Murad

He dreamt how he and his brave followers rushed at Shamil with songs and with the cry, "Hadji Murad is coming!" and how they seized him and his wifes and how he heard the wives crying and sobbing. He woke up. The song, Lya-il-allysha, and the cry "Hadji Murad is coming!" and the weeping of shamil's wives, was the howling, weeping and laughter of jackals that awoke him. Hadji Murad lifted his head, glanced at the sky which, seen between the trunks of the trees, was already growing light in the east and inquired after Khan Mahoma of a murid who sat at some distance from him. On hearing that Khan Mahoma had not yet returned, Hadji Murad again bowed his head and at once fell asleep.

He was awakened by the merry voice of Khan Mahoma returning from his mission with Bata. Khan Mahoma at once sat down beside Hadji Murad and told him how the soldiers had met them and had led them to the prince himself, and how pleased the prince was and how he promised to meet them in the morning where the Russians would be felling trees beyond the Mitchik in the Shalin glade. Bata interrupted his fellow-envoy to add details of his own.

Hadji Murad asked particularly for the words with which Vorontsov had answered his offer to go over to the russians, and Khan Mahoma and Bata replied with one voice that the prince promised to receive Hadji Murad as a guest, and to act so that it should be well for him.

Then Hadji Murad questioned them about the road, and when Khan Mahoma assured him that he knew the way well and would conduct him straight to the spot, Hadji Murad took out some money and gave Bata the promised three rubles. Then he

41

ordered his men to take out of the saddle bags his gold-ornamented weapons and his turban, and to clean themselves up so as to look well when they arrived among the Russians.

While they cleaned their weapons, harness, and horses, the stars faded away, it became quite light, and an early morning breeze sprang up.

Chapter V

Early in the morning, while it was still dark, two companies
carrying axes and commanded by Poltoratsky marched six
miles beyond the Shagirinsk Gate, and having thrown out a line
of sharpshooters set to work to fell trees as soon as the day
broke. Towards eight o'clock the mist which had mingled with
the perfumed smoke of the hissing and crackling damp green
branches on the bonfires began to rise and the wood-fellers —
who till then had not seen five paces off but had only heard one
another — began to see both the bonfires and the road through
the forest, blocked with falled trees. The sun now appeared like
a bright spot in the fog and now again was hidden.

In the glade, some way from the road, Poltoratsky, his
subaltern Tikhonov, two officers of the Third Company, and
Baron Freze, an ex-officer of the Guards and a fellow student
of Poltoratsky at the Cadet College, who had been reduced to
the ranks for fighting a duel, were sitting on drums. Bits of
paper that had contained food, cigarette stumps, and empty
bottles, lat scattered around them. The officers had had some

vodka and were now eating, and drinking porter. A drummer was uncorking their third bottle.

Poltoratsky, although he had not had enough sleep, was in that peculiar state of elation and kindly careless gaiety which he always felt when he found himself among his soldiers and with his comrades where there was a possibility of danger.

The officers were carrying on an animated conversation, the subject of which was the latest news: the death of General Sletpsov. None of them saw in this death that most important moment of a life, its termination and return to the source when it sprang — they saw in it only the valour of a gallant officer who rushed at the mountaineers sword in hand and hacked them desperately.

Though all of them — and especially those who had been in action — knew and could not help knowing that in those days in the Caucasus, and in fact anywhere and at any time, such hand-to-hand hacking as is always imagined and described never occurs (or if hacking with swords and bayonets ever does occur, it is only those who are running away that get hacked), that fiction of hand-to-hand fighting endowed them with the calm pride and cheerfulness with which they say on the drums — some with a jaunty air, others on the contrary in a very modest pose, and drank and joked without troubling about death, which might overtake them at any moment as it had overtaken Sleptsov. And in the midst of their talk, as if to confirm their expectations, they heard to the left of the road the pleasant stirring sound of a rifle shot; and a bullet, merrily whistling somewhere in the misty air, flew past and crashed into a tree.

"Hullo!" exclaimed Poltoratsky in a merry voice; "Why that's at our line. . . . There now, Kostya," and he turned to Freze, "now's your chance. Go back to the company. I will lead the whole company to support the cordon and we'll arrange a battle that will be simply delightful . . . and then we'll make a report."

Freze jumped to his feet and went at a quick pace towards the smoke-enveloped spot where he had left his company.

Poltoratsky's little Kabarda dapple-bay was brought to him, and he mounted and drew up his company and led it in the direction whence the shots were fired. The outposts stood on the skirts of the forest in front of the bare descending slope of a ravine. The wind was blowing in the direction of the forest, and not only was it possible to see the slope of the ravine, but the opposite side of it was also distinctly visible. When Poltoratsky rode up to the line the sun came out from behind the mist, and on the other side of the ravine, by the outskirts of a young forest, a few horsemen could be seen at a distance of a quarter of a mile. These were the Chechens who had pursued Hadji Murad and wanted to see him meet the Russians. One of them fired at the line. Several soldiers fired back. The Chechens retreated and the firing ceased.

But when Poltoratsky and his company came up he nevertheles gave orders to fire, and scarcely had the word been passed than along the whole line of sharpshooters the incessant, merry, stirring rattle of our rifles began, acompanied by pretty dissolving cloudlets of smoke. The soldiers, pleased to have some distraction, hastened to load and fired shot after shot. The Chechens evidently caught the feeling of excitement, and leaping forward one after another fired a few shots at our men.

One of these shots wounded a soldier. It was the same Avdeev who had lain in ambush the night before.

When his comrades approached him he was lying prone, holding his wounded stomach with both hands, and rocking himself with a rhythmic motion moaned softly. He belonged to Poltoratsky's company, and Poltoratsky, seeing a group of soldiers collected, rode up to them.

"What is it, lad? Been hit?" said Poltoratsky. "Where?"

Avdeev did not answer.

"I was just going to load, your honor, when I heard a click," said a soldier who had been with Avdeef; "and I look and see he's dropped his gun."

"Tut, tut, tut!" Poltoratsky clicked his tongue. "Does it hurt much, Avdeev?"

"It doesn't hurt but it stops me walking. A dropu of vodka now, your honor!"

Some vodka (or rather the spirit drunk by the soldiers in the Caucasus) was found, and Panov, severely frowning, brought Avdeev a can-lid full. Avdeev tried to drink it but immediately handed back the lid.

"My soul truns against it," he said. "Drink it yourself."

Panov drank up the spirit.

Avdeev raised himself but sank back at once. They spread out a cloak and laid him on it.

"Your honor, the colonel is coming," said the sergeant-major to Poltoratsky.

"All right. then will you see to him?" said Poltoratsky, and flourishing his whip he rode at a fast trot to meet Vorontsov.

Vorontsov was riding his thoroughbred English chestnut gelding, and was accompanied by the adjutant, a Cossack, and a Chechen interpreter.

"What's happening here?" asked Vorontsov.

"Why, a skirmishing party attacked our advanced line," Poltoratsky answered.

"Come, come — you arranged the whole thing yourself!"

"Oh no, Prince, not I," said Poltoratsky with a smile; "they pushed forward of their own accord."

"I hear a soldier has been wounded?"

"Yes, it's a great pity. He's a good soldier."

"Seriously?"

"Seriously, I believe . . . in the stomach."

"And do you know where I am going?" vorontsov asked.

47

"I don't."

"Can't you guess?"

"No."

"Hadji Murad has surrendered and we are now going to meet him."

"You don't mean to say so?"

"His envoy came to me yesterday," said Vorontsov, with difficulty repressing a smile of pleasure. "He will be waiting for me at the Shalin glade in a few minutes. Place sharpshooters as far as the glade, and then come and join me."

"I understand," said Poltoratsky, lifting his hand to his cap, and rode back to his company. He led the sharp shooters to the right himself, and ordered the seargeant-major to do the same on the left side.

The wounded Avdeev had meanwhile been taken back to the fort by some of the soldiers.

On his way back to rejoin vorontsov, Poltoratsky noticed behind him several horsemen who were overtaking him. In front on a white-maned horse rode a man of imposing appearance. He wore a turban and carried weapons with gold ornaments. This man was Hadji Murad. He approached Poltoratsky and said something to him in Tartar. Raising his eyebrows, Poltoratsky made a gesture with his arms to show that he did not understand, and smiled. Hadji Murad gave him smile for smile, and that smile struck Poltoratsky by its childlike kindliness. Poltoratsky had never expected to see the terrible mountain chief look like that. He had expected to see a morose, hard-featured man, and here was a vivacious person whose smile was so kindly that Poltoratsky felt as if he were an old acquaintance. He had only one peculiarity: his eyes, set wide apart, which gazed from under their black brows calmly, attentively, and penetratingly into the eyes of others.

Hadji Murad's suit consisted of five men, among them was Khan Mahoma, who had been to see Prince Vorontsov that night. He was a rosy, round-faced fellow with black lashless eyes and a beaming expression, full of the joy of life. Then there was the Avar Khanefi, a thick-set, hairy man, whose eyebrows met. He was in charge of all Hadji Murad's property and led a stud-bred horse which carried tightly packed saddle bags. Two men of the suite were particularly striking. The first was a Lesghian: a youth, broad-shouldered but with a waist as slim as a woman's, beautiful ram-like eyes, and the beginnings of a brown beard. This was Eldar. The other, Gamzalo, was a Chechen with a short red beard and no eyebrows or eyelashes; he was blind in one eye and had a scar across his nose and face. Poltoratsky pointed out Vorontsov, who had just appeared on the road. Hadji Murad rode to meet him, and putting his right hand on his heart said something in Tartar and stopped. The Chechen interpreter translated.

"He says, 'I surrender myself to the will of the Russian Tsar. I wish to serve him,' he says. 'I wished to so do long ago but Shamil would not let me.'"

Having heard what the interpreter said, Vorontsov stretched out his hand in its wash-leather glove to Hadji Murad. Hadji Murad looked at it hestitatingly for a moment and then pressed it firmly, again saying something and looking first at the interpreter and then at Vorontsov.

"He says he did not wish to surrender to any one but you, as you are the son of the Sirdar and he respects you much."

Vorontsov nodded to express his thanks. Hadji Murad again said something, pointing to his suite.

"He says that these men, his henchmen, will serve the Russians as well as he."

Vorontsov turned towards then and nodded to them too. The merry, black-eyed, lashless Chechen, Khan Mahoma, also nodded and said something which was probably amusing, for the hairy Avar drew his lips into a smile, showing his ivory-white teeth. But the red-haired Gamzalo's one red eye just glanced at Vorontsov and then was again fixed on the ears of his horse.

When Vorontsov and Hadji Murad with their retinues rode back to the fort the soldiers released form the lines gathered in groups and made their own comments.

"What a lot of men that damned fellow has destroyed! And now see what a fuss they will make of him!"

"Naturally. He was Shamil's right hand, and now — no fear!"

"Still there's no denying it! he's a fine fellow — a regular dzhigit!"

"And the red one! He squints at you like a beast!"

"Ugh! He must be a hound!"

They had all specially noticed the red one. Where the wood-felling was going on the soldiers nearest to the road ran out to look. Their officer shouted to them, but Vorontsov stopped him.

"Let them have a look at their old friend."

"You know who that is?" he added, turning to the nearest soldier, and speaking the words slowly with his English accent.

"No, your Excellency."

"Hadji Murad. . . . Heard of him?"

"How could we help it, your Excellency? We've beaten him many a time!"

"Yes, and we've had it hot from him too."

"Yes, that's true, your Excellency," answered the soldier, pleased to be talking with his chief.

Hadji Murad understood that they were speaking about him, and smiled brightly with his eyes.

Vornotsov returned to the fort in a very cheerful mood.

Leo Tolstoy

Chapter VI

Young Vorontsov was much pleased that it was he, and no one else, who had succeeded in winning over and receiving Hadji Murad — next to Shamil Russia's chief and most active enemy. There was only one unpleasant thing about it: General Meller-Zakomelsky was in command of the army at Vozdvizhenski, and the whole affair ought to have been carried out through him. As Vorontsov had done everything himself without reporting it there might be some unpleasantness, and this thought rather interfered with his satisfaction. On reaching his house he entrusted Hadji Murad's henchmen to the regimental adjutant and himself showed Hadji Murad into the house.

Princess Marya Vasilevna, elegantly dressed and smiling, and her little son, a handsome curly-headed child of six, met Hadji Murad in the drawing room. The latter placed his hands on his heart, and through the interpreter — who had entered with him — said with solemnity that he regarded himself as the prince's kunak, since the prince had brought him into his own house; and that a kunak's whole family was as sacred as the kunak himself.

Hadji Murad's appearance and manners pleased Marya Vasilevna, and the fact that he flushed when she held out her large white hand to him inclined her still more in his favor. She invited him to sit down, and having asked him whether he drank coffee, had some served. He, however, declined it when it came. He understood a little Russian but could not speak it. When something was said which he could not understand he smiled, and his smile pleased Marya Vasilevna just as it had pleased Poltoratsky. The curly-haired, keen-eyed little boy (whom his mother called Bulka) standing beside her did not take his eyes off Hadji Murad, whom he had always heard spoken of as a great warrior.

Leaving Hadji Murad with his wife, Vorontsov went to his office to do what was necessary about reporting the fact of Hadji Murad's having cove over to the Russians. When he had written a report to the general in command of the left flank — General Kozlovsky — at Grozny, and a letter to his father, Vorontsov hurried home, afraid that his wife might be vexed with him for forcing on her this terrible stranger, who had to be treated in such a way that he should not take offense, and yet not too kindly. But his fears were needless. Hadji Murad was sitting in an armchair with little Bulka, Vorontsov's stepson, on his knee, and with bent head was listening attentively to the interpreter who was translating to him the words of the laughing marya Vasilevna. Marya Vasilevna was telling him that if every time a kunak admired anything of his he made him a present of it, he would soon have to go about like Adam. . . .

When the prince entered, Hadji Murad rose at once and, surprising and offending Bulka by putting him off his knee, changed the playful expression of his face to a stern and serious one. He only sat down again when Vorontsov had himself taken a seat.

Continuing the conversation he answered Marya Vasilevna by telling her that it was a law among his people that anything your kunak admired must be presented to him.

"Thy son, kunak?" he said in Russian, patting the curly head of the boy who had again climbed on his knee.

"He is delightful, your brigand!" said Marya Vasilevna to her husband in french. "Bulka has been admiring his dagger, and he has given it to him."

Bulka showed the dagger to his father. "C'est un objet de prix!" added she.

"Il faudra trouver l'occasion de lui faire cadeau," said Vorontsov.

Hadji Murad, his eyes turned down, sat stroking the boy's curly hair and saying: "Dzhigit, dzhigit!"

"A beautiful, beautiful dagger," said Vorontsov, half drawing out the sharpened blade which had a ridge down the center. "I thank thee!"

"Ask him what I can do for him," he said to the interpreter.

The interpreter translated, and Hadji Murad at once replied that he wanted nothing but that he begged to be taken to a place where he could say his prayers.

Vorontsov called his valet and told him to do what Hadji Murad desired.

As soon as Hadji Murad was alone in the room allotted to him his face altered. The pleased expression, now kindly and now stately, vanished, and a look of anxiety showed itself. Vorontsov had received him far better than Hadji Murad had expected. But the better the reception the less did Hadji Murad trust Vorontsov and his officers. He feared everything: that he might be seized, chained, and sent to Siberia, or simply killed; and therefore he was on his guard. He asked Eldar, when the latter entered his room, where his murids had been put and whether their arms had been taken from them, and where the horses were. Eldar reported that the horses were in the prince's stables; that the men had been placed in a barn; that they retained their arms, and that the interpreter was giving them food and tea.

Hadji Murad shook his head in doubt, and after undressing said his prayers and told Eldar to bring him his silver dagger. He then dressed, and having fastened his belt, sat down on the divan with his legs tucked under him, to await what might befall him.

At four in the afternoon the interpreter came to call him to dine with the prince.

At dinner he hardly ate anything except some pilau, to which he helped himself from the very part of the dish from which Marya Vasilevna had helped herself.

"He is afraid we shall poison him," Marya Vasilevna remarked to her husband. "He has helped himself from the place where I took my helping." Then instantly turning to Hadji Murad she asked him through the interpreter when he would pray again. Hadji Murad lifted five fingers and pointed to the sun. "Then it will soon be time," and Vorontsov drew out his watch and pressed a spring. The watch struck four and one quarter. This evidently surprised Hadji Murad, and he asked to hear it again and to be allowed to look at the watch.

"Voila l'occasion! Donnez-lui la montre," said the princess to her husband.

Vorontsov at once offered the watch to Hadji Murad.

The latter placed his hand on his breast and took the watch. He touched the spring several times, listened, and nodded his head approvingly.

After dinner, Meller-Zakomelsky's aide-de-camp was announced.

The aide-de-camp informed the prince that the general, having heard of Hadji Murad's arrival, was highly displeased that this had not been reported to him, and required Hadji Murad to be brought to him without delay. Vorontsov replied that the general's command should be obeyed, and through the interpreter informed Hadji Murad of these orders and asked him to go to Meller with him.

When Marya Vasilevna heard what the aide-de-camp had come about, she at once understood that unpleasantness might arise between her husband and the general, and in spite of all her husband's attempts to dissuade her, decided to go with him and Hadji Murad.

"Vous feriez blen mieux de rester — c'est mon affaire, non pas la votre. . . ."

"Vous ne pouvez pas m'empecher d'aller voir madame la generale!"

"You could go some other time."

"But I wish to go now!"

There was no help for it, so Vorontsov agreed, and they all three went.

When they entered, Meller with somber politeness conducted Marya Vasilevna to his wife and told his aide-de-camp to show Hadji Murad to the waiting room and not let him out till further orders.

"Please . . . " he said to Vorontsov, opening the door of his study and letting the prince enter before him.

Having entered the study he stopped in front of Vorontsov and, without offering him a seat, said:

"I am in command here and therefore all negotiations with the enemy have to be carried on through me! Why did you not report to me that Hadji Murad had come over?"

"An emissary came to me and announced his wish to capitulate only to me," replied Vorontsov growing pale with excitement, expecting some rude expression from the angry general and at the same time becoming infected with his anger.

"I ask you why was I not informed?"

"I intended to inform you, Baron, but . . . "

"You are not to address me as 'Baron,' but as 'Your Excellency'!" And here the baron's pent-up irritation suddenly broke out and he uttered all that had long been boiling in his soul.

"I have not served my sovereign twenty-seven years in order that men who began their service yesterday, relying on family connections, should give orders under my very nose about matters that do not concern them!"

"Your Excellency, I request you not to say things that are incorrect!" interrupted Vorontsov.

"I am saying what is correct, and I won't allow . . . " said the general, still more irritably.

But at that moment Marya Vasilevna entered, rustling with her skirts and followed by a model-looking little lady, Meller-Zakomelsky's wife.

"Come, come, Baron! Simon did not wish to displease you," began Marya Vasilevna.

"I am not speaking about that, Princess. . . . "

"Well, well, let's forget it all! . . . You know, 'A bad peace is better than a good quarrel!' . . . Oh dear, what am I saying?" and she laughed.

The angry general capitulated to the enchanting laugh of the beauty. A smile hovered under his moustache.

"I confess I was wrong," said Vorontsov, "but—"

"And I too got rather carried away," said Meller, and held out his hand to the prince.

Peace was re-established, and it was decided to leave Hadji Murad with the general for the present, and then to send him to the commander of the left flank.

Hadji Murad sat in the next room and though he did not understand what was said, he understood what it was necessary for him to understand — namely, that they were quarrelling about him, that his desertion of Shamil was a matter of immense importance to the Russians, and that therefore not only would they not exile or kill him, but that he would be able to demand much from them. He also understood that though Meller-Zakomelsky was the commanding officer, he had not as much influence as his subordinate Vorontsov, and that Vorontsov was important and Meller-Zakomelsky unimportant; and therefore when Meller-Zakomelsky sent for him and began to question him, Hadji Murad bore himself proudly and ceremoniously, saying that he had come from the mountains to serve the White Tsar and would give account only to his Sirdar, meaning the commander-in-chief, Prince Vorontsov senior, in Tiflis.

Chapter VII

The wounded Avdeev was taken to the hospital — a small wooden building roofed with boards at the entrance of the fort — and was placed on one of the empty beds in the common ward. There were four patients in the ward: one ill with typhus and in high fever; another, pale, with dark shadows under his eyes, who had ague, was just expecting attack and yawned continually; and two more who had been wounded in a raid three weeks before: one in the hand — he was up — and the other in the shoulder. The latter was sitting on a bed. All of them except the typhus patient surrounded and questioned the newcomer and those who had brought him.

"Sometimes they fire as if they were spilling peas over you, and nothing happens . . . and this time only about five shots were fired," related one of the bearers.

"Each man get what fate sends!"

"Oh!" groaned Avdeev loudly, trying to master his pain when they began to place him on the bed; but he stopped groaning when he was on it, and only frowned and moved his feet

61

continually. He held his hands over his wound and looked fixedly before him.

The doctor came, and gave orders to turn the wounded man over to see whether the bullet had passed out behind.

"What's this?" the doctor asked, pointing to the large white scars that crossed one another on the patient's back and loins.

"That was done long ago, your honor!" replied Avdeev with a groan.

They were scars left by the flogging Avdeev had received for the money he drank.

Avdeev was again turned over, and the doctor probed in his stomach for a long time and found the bullet, but failed to extract it. He put a dressing on the wound, and having stuck plaster over it went away. During the whole time the doctor was probing and bandaging the wound Avdeev lay with clenched teeth and closed eyes, but when the doctor had gone he opened them and looked around as though amazed. His eyes were turned on the other patients and on the surgeon's orderly, though he seemed to see not them but something else that surprised him.

His friends Panov and Serogin came in, but Avdeev continued to lie in the same position looking before him with surprise. It was long before he recognized his comrades, though his eyes gazed straight at them.

"I say, Peter, have you no message to send home?" said Panov.

Avdeev did not answer, though he was looking Panov in the face.

"I say, haven't you any orders to send home?" again repeated Panov, touching Avdeev's cold, large-boned hand.

Avdeev seemed to come to.

"Ah! . . . Panov!"

"Yes, I'm here. . . . I've come! Have you nothing for home? Serogin would write a letter."

"Serogin . . . " said Avdeev moving his eyes with difficulty towards Serogin, "will you write? . . . Well then, wrote so: 'Your son,' say 'Peter, has given orders that you should live long. He envied his brother' . . . I told you about that today . . . ' and now he is himself glad. Don't worry him. . . . Let him live. God grant it him. I am glad!' Write that."

Having said this he was silent for some time with his eyes fixed on Panov.

"And did you find your pipe?" he suddenly asked.

Panov did not reply.

"Your pipe . . . your pipe! I mean, have you found it?" Avdeev repeated.

"It was in my gag."

"That's right! . . . Well, and now give me a candle to hold . . . I am going to die," said Avdeev.

Just then Poltoratsky came in to inquire after his soldier.

"How goes it, my lad! Badly?" said he.

Avdeev closed his eyes and shook his head negatively. His broad-cheeked face was pale and stern. He did not reply, but again said to Panov:

"Bring a candle. . . . I am going to die."

A wax taper was placed in his hand but his fingers would not bend, so it was placed between them and held up for him.

Poltoratsky went away, and five minutes later the orderly put his ear to Avdeev's heart and said that all was over.

Avdeev's death was described in the following manner in the report sent to Tiflis:

"23rd Nov. — Two companies of the Kurin regiment advanced from the fort on a wood-felling expedition. At mid-day a considerable number of mountaineers suddenly attacked the wood-fellers. The sharpshooters began to retreat, but the 2nd Company charged with the bayonet and overthrew the mountaineers. In this affair two privates were slightly wounded and one killed. The mountaineers lost about a hundred men killed and wounded."

Chapter VIII

On the day Peter Avdeev died in the hospital at Vozdvizhensk, his old father with the wife of the brother in whose stead he had enlisted, and that brother's daughter — who was already approaching womanhood and almost of age to get married — were threshing oats on the hard-frozen threshing floor.

There had been a heavy fall of snow the previous night followed towards morning by a severe front. The old man woke when the cocks were crowing for the third time, and seeing the bright moonlight through the frozen windowpanes got down from the stove, put on his boots, his sheepskin coat and cap, and went out to the threshing floor. Having worked there for a couple of hours he returned to the hut and awoke his son and the women. When the woman and girl came to the threshing floor they found it ready swept, with a wooden shovel sticking in the dry white snow, beside which were birch brooms with the twigs upwards and two rows of oat sheaves laid ears to ears in a long line the whole length of the clean threshing floor. They chose their flails and started threshing, keeping time with their triple blows. The old man struck powerfully with his heavy flail, breaking the straw, the girl struck the ears from above with measured blows, and the daughter-in-law turned the oats over with her flail.

The moon had set, dawn was breaking, and they were finishing the line of sheaves when Akim, the eldest son, in his sheepskin and cap, joined the threshers.

"What are you lazing about for?" shouted his father to him, pausing in his work and leaning on his flail.

"The horses had to be seen to."

"'Horses seen to!'" the father repeated, mimicking him. "The old woman will look after them. . . . Take your flail! You're getting too fat, you drunkard!"

"Have you been standing me treat?" muttered the son.

"What?" said the old man, frowning sternly and missing a stroke.

The son silently took a flail and they began threshing with four flails.

"Trak, tapatam . . . trak, tapatam . . . trak . . . " came down the old man's heavy flail after the three others.

"Why, you've got a nape like a goodly gentleman! . . . Look here, my trousers have hardly anything to hand on!" said the old man, omitting his stroke and only swinging his flail in the air so as not to get out of time.

They had finished the row, and the women began removing the straw with rakes.

"Peter was a fool to go in your stead. They'd have knocked the nonsense out of you in the army, and he was worth five of such as you at home!"

"That's enough, father," said the daughter-in-law, as she threw aside the binders that had come off the sheaves.

"Yes, feed the six of you and get no work out of a single one! Peter used to work for two. He was not like . . . "

Along the trodden path from the house came the old man's wife, the frozen snow creaking under the new bark shoes she wore over her tightly wound woolen leg-bands. The men were shovelling the unwinnowed grain into heaps, the woman and the girl sweeping up what remained.

The Elder has been and orders everybody to go and work for the master, carting bricks," said the old woman. "I've got breakfast ready. . . . Come along, won't you?"

"All right. . . . Harness the roan and go," said the old man to Akim, "and you'd better look out that you don't get me into trouble as you did the other day! . . . I can't help regretting Peter!"

"When he was at home you used to scold him," retorted Akim. "Now he's away you keep nagging at me."

"That shows you deserve it," said his mother in the same angry tones. "You'll never be Peter's equal."

"Oh, all right," said the son.

"'All right,' indeed! You've drunk the meal, and now you say 'all right!'"

"Let bygones be bygones!" said the daughter-in-law.

The disagreements between father and son had begun long ago — almost from the time Peter went as a soldier. Even then the old man felt that he had parted with an eagle for a cuckoo. It is true that it was right — as the old man understood it — for a childless man to go in place of a family man. Akin had four children and Peter had none; but Peter was a worker like his father, skilful, observant, strong, enduring, and above all industrious. He was always at work. If he happened to pass by where people were working he lent a helping hand as his father would have done, and took a turn or two with the scythe, or loaded a cart, or felled a tree, or chopped some wood. The old man regretted his going away, but there was no help for it. Conscription in those days was like death. A soldier was a severed branch, and to think about him at home was to tear one's heart uselessly. Only occasionally, to prick his elder son, did the father mention him, as he had done that day. But his mother often thought of her younger son, and for a long time — more than a year now — she had been asking her husband to send Peter a little money, but the old man had made no response.

The Kurenkovs were a well-to-do family and the old man had some savings hidden away, but he would on no account have consented to touch what he had laid by. Now however the old woman having heard him mention their younger son, made up her mind to ask him again to send him at least a ruble after selling the oats. This she did. As soon as the young people had gone to work for the proprietor and the old folks were left alone together, she persuaded him to send Peter a ruble out of the oats-money.

So when ninety-six bushels of the winnowed oats had been packed onto three sledges lined with sacking carefully pinned together at the top with wooden skewers, she gave her husband a letter the church clerk had written at her dictation, and the old man promised when he got to town to enclose a ruble and send it off to the right address.

The old man, dressed in a new sheepskin with homespun cloak over it, his legs wrapped round with warm white woollen leg-bands, took the letter, placed it in his wallet, said a prayer, got into the front sledge, and drove to town. His grandson drove in the last sledge. When he reached town the old man asked the innkeeper to read the letter to him, and listened to it attentively and approvingly.

In her letter Peter's mother first sent him her blessing, then greetings from everybody and the news of his godfather's death, and at the end she added that Aksinya (Peter's wife) had not wished to stay with them but had gone into service, where they heard she was living honestly and well. Then came a reference to the present of a ruble, and finally a message which the old woman, yielding to her sorrows, had dictated with tears in her eyes and the church clerk had taken down exactly, word for word:

"One thing more, my darling child, my sweet dove, my own Peterkin! I have wept my eyes out lamenting for thee, thou

light of my eyes. To whom has thou left me? . . . " At this point
the old woman had sobbed and wept, and said: "That will do!"
So the words stood in the letter; but it was not fated that Peter
should receive the news of his wife's having left home, nor the
present of the ruble, nor his mother's last words. The letter
with the money in it came back with the announcement that
Peter had been killed in the war, "defending his Tsar, his
Fatherland, and the Orthodox Faith." That is how the army
clerk expressed it.

The old woman, when this news reached her, wept for as long
as she could spare time, and then set to work again. The very
next Sunday she went to church and had a requiem chanted and
Peter's name entered among those for whose souls prayers
were to be said, and she distributed bits of holy bread to all the
good people in memory of Peter, the servant of God.

Aksinya, his widow, also lamented loudly when she heard of
the death of her beloved husband with whom she had lived but
one short year. She regretted her husband and her own ruined
life, and in her lamentations mentioned Peter's brown locks
and his love, and the sadness of her life with her little orphaned
Vanka, and bitterly reproached Peter for having had pity on his
brother but none on her — obliged to wander among strangers!

But in the depth of her soul Aksinya was glad of her husband's
death. She was pregnant a second time by the shopman with
whom she was living, and no one would now have a right to
scold her, and the shopman could marry her as he had said he
would when he was persuading her to yield.

Chapter IX

Michael Semenovich Vorontsov, being the son of the Russian
Ambassador, had been educated in England and possessed a
European education quite exceptional among the higher
Russian officials of his day. He was ambitious, gentle and kind
in his manner with inferiors, and a finished courtier with
superiors. He did not understand life without power and
submission. He had obtained all the highest ranks and
decorations and was looked upon as a clever commander, and
even as the conqueror of Napoleon at Krasnoe.

In 1852 he was over seventy, but young for his age, he moved
briskly, and above all was in full possession of a facile, refined,
and agreeable intellect which he used to maintain his power
and strengthen and increase his popularity. He possessed large
means — his own and his wife's (who had been a countess
Branitski) — and received an enormous salary as Viceroy, and
he spent a great part of his means on building a palace and
laying out a garden on the south coast of the Crimea.

On the evening of December the 4th, 1852, a courier's troika
drew up before his palace in Tiflis. an officer, tired and black

with dust, sent by General Kozlovski with the news of Hadji Murad's surrender to the Russians, entered the wide porch, stretching the stiffened muscles of his legs as he passed the sentinel. It was six o'clock, and Vorontsov was just going in to dinner when he was informed of the courier's arrival. He received him at once, and was therefore a few minutes late for dinner.

When he entered the drawing room the thirty persons invited to dine, who were sitting beside Princess Elizabeth Ksaverevna Vorontsova, or standing in groups by the windows, turned their faces towards him. Vorontsov was dressed in his usual black military coat, with shoulderstraps but no epaulets, and wore the White Cross of the Order of St. George at his neck.

His clean shaven, foxlike face wore a pleasant smile as, screwing up his eyes, he surveyed the assembly. Entering with quick soft steps he apologized to the ladies for being late, greeted the men, and approaching Princess Manana Orbelyani — a tall, fine, handsome woman of Oriental type about forty-five years of age — he offered her his arm to take her in to dinner. Princess Elizabeth Ksaverevna Vorontsova gave her arm to a red-haired general with bristly mustaches who was visiting Tiflis. A Georgian prince offered his arm to Princess Vorontsova's friend, Countess Choiseuil. Doctor Andreevsky, the aide-de-camp, and others, with ladies or without, followed these first couples. Footmen in livery and knee-breeches drew back and replaced the guests' chairs when they sat down, while the major-domo ceremoniously ladled out steaming soup from a silver tureen.

Vorontsov took his place in the center of one side of the long table, and wife sat opposite, with the general on her right. On the prince's right sat his lady, the beautiful Orbelyani; and on his left was a graceful, dark, red-cheeked Georgian woman, glittering with jewels and incessantly smiling.

"Excellentes, chere amie!" replied Vorontsov to his wife's inquiry about what news the courier had brought him. "Simon a eu de la chance!" And he began to tell aloud, so that everyone could hear, the striking news (for him alone not quite unexpected, because negotiations had long been going on) that Hadji Murad, the bravest and most famous of Shamil's officers, had come over to the Russians and would in a day or two be brought to Tiflis.

Everybody — even the young aides-de-camp and officials who sat at the far ends of the table and who had been quietly laughing at something among themselves — became silent and listened.

"And you, General, have you ever met this Hadji Murad?" asked the princess of her neighbor, the carroty general with the bristly mustaches, when the prince had finished speaking.

"More than once, Princess."

And the general went on to tell how Hadji Murad, after the mountaineers had captured Gergebel in 1843, had fallen upon General Pahlen's detachment and killed Colones Zolotukhin almost before their very eyes.

Vorontsov listened to the general and smiled amiably, evidently pleased that the latter had joined in the conversation. But suddenly his face assumed an absent-minded and depressed expression.

The general, having started talking, had begun to tell of his second encounter with Hadji Murad.

"Why, it was he, if your Excellency will please remember," said the general, "who arranged the ambush that attacked the rescue party in the 'Biscuit' expedition."

"Where?" asked Vorontsov, screwing up his eyes.

What the brave general spoke of as the "rescue" was the affair in the unfortunate Dargo campaign in which a whole detachment, including Prince Vorontsov who commanded it, would certainly have perished had it not been rescued by the arrival of fresh troops. Every one knew that the whole Dargo campaign under Vorontsov's command — in which the Russians lost many killed and wounded and several cannon — had been a shameful affair, and therefore if any one mentioned it in Vorontsov's presence they did so only in the aspect in which Vorontsov had reported it to the Tsar — as a brilliant achievement of the Russian army. But the word "rescue" plainly indicated that it was not a brilliant victory but a blunder costing many lives. Everybody understood this and some pretended not to notice the meaning of the general's words, others nervously waited to see what would follow, while a few exchanged glances, and smiled. Only the carroty general with the bristly mustaches noticed nothing, and carried away by his narrative quietly replied:

"At the rescue, your Excellency."

Having started on his favorite theme, the general recounted circumstantially how Hadji Murad had so cleverly cut the detachment in two that if the rescue party had not arrived (he seemed to be particularly fond of repeating the word "rescue") not a man in the division would have escaped, because . . . He did not finish his story, for Manana Orbelyani, having understood what was happening, interrupted him by asking if he had found comfortable quarters in Tiflis. The general, surprised, glanced at everybody all round and saw his aides-de-camp from the end of the table looking fixedly and significantly at him, and he suddenly understood! Without replying to the princess's question, he frowned, became silent, and began hurriedly swallowing the delicacy that lay on his plate, the appearance and taste of which both completely mystified him.

Everybody felt uncomfortable, but the awkwardness of the situation was relieved by the Georgian prince — a very stupid man but an extraordinarily refined and artful flatterer and courtier — who sat on the other side of Princess Vorontsova. Without seeming to have noticed anything he began to relate how Hadji Murad had carried off the widow of Akhmet Khan of Mekhtuli.

"He came into the village at night, seized what he wanted, and galloped off again with the whole party."

"Why did he want that particular woman?" asked the princess.

"Oh, he was her husband's enemy, and pursued him but could never once succeed in meeting him right up to the time of his death, so he revenged himself on the widow."

The princess translated this into French for her old friend Countess Choiseuil, who sat next to the Georgian prince.

"Quelle horreur!" said the countess, closing her eyes and shaking her head.

"Oh no!" said Vorontsov, smiling. "I have been told that he treated his captive with chivalrous respect and afterwards released her."

"Yes, for a ransom!"

"Well, of course. But all the same he acted honorably."

These words of Vorontsov's set the tone for the further conversation. The courtiers understood that the more importance was attributed to Hadji Murad the better the prince would be pleased.

"The man's audacity is amazing. A remarkable man!"

"Why, in 1849 he dashed into Temir Khan Shura and plundered the shops in broad daylight."

An Armenian sitting at the end of the table, who had been in Temir Khan Shura at the time, related the particulars of that exploit of Hadji Murad's.

In fact, Hadji Murad was the sole topic of conversation during the whole dinner.

Everybody in succession praised his courage, his ability, and his magnanimity. Someone mentioned his having ordered twenty six prisoners to be killed, but that too was met by the usual rejoinder, "What's to be done? A la guerre, comme al la guerre!"

"He is a great man."

"Had he been born in Europe he might have been another Napoleon," said the stupid Georgian prince with a gift of flattery.

He knew that every mention of Napoleon was pleasant to Vorontsov, who wore the White Cross at his neck as a reward for having defeated him.

"Well, not Napoleon perhaps, but a gallant cavalry general if you like," said Vorontsov.

"If not Napoleon, then Murat."

"And his name is Hadji Murad!"

"Hadji Murad has surrendered and now there'll be an end to Shamil too," someone remarked.

"They feel that now" (this "now" meant under Vorontsov) "they can't hold out," remarked another.

"Tout cela est grace a vous!" said Manana Orbelyani.

Prince Vorontsov tried to moderate the waves of flattery which began to flow over him. Still, it was pleasant, and in the best of spirits he led his lady back into the drawing room.

After dinner, when coffee was being served in the drawing room, the prince was particularly amiable to everybody, and going up to the general with the red bristly mustaches he tried to appear not to have noticed his blunder.

Having made a round of the visitors he sat down to the card table. He only played the old-fashioned game of ombre. His partners were the Georgian prince, an Armenia general (who had learned the game of ombre from Prince Vorontsov's valet), and Doctor Andreevsky, a man remarkable for the great influence he exercised.

Placing beside him his gold snuff-box with a portrait of Aleksandr I on the lid, the prince tore open a pack of highly glazed cards and was going to spread them out, when his Italian valet brought him a letter on a silver tray.

"Another courier, your Excellency."

Vorontsov laid down the cards, excused himself, opened the letter, and began to read.

The letter was from his son, who described Hadji Murad's surrender and his own encounter with Meller-Zakomelsky.

The princess came up and inquired what their son had written.

"It's all about the same matter. . . . Il a eu quelques desagrements avec le commandant de la place. Simon a eu tort. . . . But 'All's well that ends well,'" he added in English, handing the letter to his wife; and turning to his respectfully waiting partners he asked them to draw cards.

When the first round had been dealt Vorontsov did what he
was in the habit of doing when in a particularly pleasant mood:
with his white, wrinkled old hand he took out a pinch of French
snuff, carried it to his nose, and released it.

Leo Tolstoy

Chapter X

When Hadji Murad appeared at the prince's palace next day,
the waiting room was already full of people. Yesterday's
general with the bristly mustaches was there in full uniform
with all his decorations, having come to take leave. There was
the commander of a regiment who was in danger of being court
martialled for misappropriating commisarriat money, and there
was a rich Armenian (patronized by Doctor Andreevsky) who
wanted to obtain from the Government a renewal of his
monopoly for the sale of vodka. There, dressed in black, was
the widow of an officer who had been killed in action. She had
come to ask for a pension, or for free education for her
children. There was a ruined Georgian prince in a magnificent
Georgian costume who was trying to obtain for himself some
confiscated Church property. There was an official with a large
roll of paper containing a new plan for subjugating the
Caucasus. There was also a Khan who had come solely to be
able to tell his people at home that he had called on the prince.

They all waited their turn and were one by one shown into the
prince's cabinet and out again by the aide-de-camp, a
handsome, fair-haired youth.

When Hadji Murad entered the waiting room with his brisk
though limping step all eyes were turned towards him and he
heard his name whispered from various parts of the room.

He was dressed in a long white Circassian coat over a brown
beshmet trimmed round the collar with fine silver lace. He
wore black leggings and soft shoes of the same color which
were stretched over his instep as tight as gloves. On his head he
wore a high cap draped turban-fashion — that same turban for
which, on the denunciation of Akhmet Khan, he had been
arrested by General Klugenau and which had been the cause of
his going over to Shamil.

He stepped briskly across the parquet floor of the waiting
room, his whole slender figure swaying slightly in consequence
of his lameness in one leg which was shorter than the other.
His eyes, set far apart, looked calmly before him and seemed to
see no one.

The handsome aide-de-camp, having greeted him, asked him to
take a seat while he went to announce him to the prince, but
Hadji Murad declined to sit down and, putting his hand on his
dagger, stood with one foot advanced, looking round
contemptuously at all those present.

The prince's interpreter, Prince Tarkhanov, approached Hadji
Murad and spoke to him. Hadji Murad answered abruptly and
unwillingly. A Kumyk prince, who was there to lodge a
complaint against a police official, came out of the prince's
room, and then the aide-de-camp called Hadji Murad, led him
to the door of the cabinet, and showed him in.

Hadji Murad

The Commander-in-Chief received Hadji Murad standing beside his table, and his old white face did not wear yesterday's smile but was rather stern and solemn.

On entering the large room with its enormous table and great windows with green venetian blinds, Hadji Murad placed his small sunburnt hands on his chest just where the front of his white coat overlapped, and lowering his eyes began, without hurrying, to speak distinctly and respectfully, using the Kumyk dialect which he spoke well.

"I place myself under the powerful protection of the great Tsar and of yourself," said he, "and promise to serve the White Tsar in faith and truth to the last drop of my blood, and I hope to be useful to you in the war with Shamil who is my enemy and yours."

Having the interpreter out, Vorontsov glanced at Hadji Murad and Hadji Murad glanced at Vorontsov.

The eyes of the two men met, and expressed to each other much that could not have been put into words and that was not at all what the interpreter said. Without words they told each other the whole truth. Vorontsov's eyes said that he did not believe a single word Hadji Murad was saying, and that he knew he was and always would be an enemy to everything Russian and had surrendered only because he was obliged to. Hadji Murad understood this and yet continued to give assurances of his fidelity. His eyes said, "That old man ought to be thinking of his death and not of war, but though he is old he is cunning, and I must be careful." Vorontsov understood this also, but nevertheless spoke to Hadji Murad in the way he considered necessary for the success of the war.

"Tell him," said Vorontsov, "that our sovereign is as merciful as he is mighty and will probably at my request pardon him and take him into his service. . . . Have you told him?" he asked looking at Hadji Murad. . . . "Until I receive my master's gracious decision, tell him I take it on myself to receive him and make his sojourn among us pleasant."

Hadji Murad again pressed his hands to the center of his chest and began to say something with animation.

"He says," the interpreter translated, "that formerly, when he governed Avaria in 1839, he served the Russians faithfully and would never have deserted them had not his enemy, Akhmet Khan, wishing to ruin him, calumniated him to General Klugenau."

"I know, I know," said Vorontsov (though if he had ever known he had long forgotten it). "I know," he repeated, sitting down and motioning Hadji Murad to the divan that stood beside the wall. But Hadji Murad did not sit down. Shrugging his powerful shoulders as a sign that he could not bring himself to sit in the presence of so important a man, he went on, addressing the interpreter:

"Akhmet Khan and Shamil are both my enemies. Tell the prince that Akhmet Khan is dead and I cannot revenge myself on him, but Shamil lives and I will not die without taking vengeance on him," said he, knitting his brows and tightly closing his mouth.

"Yes, yes; but how does he want to revenge himself on Shamil?" said Vorontsov quietly to the interpreter. "And tell him he may sit down."

Hadji Murad again declined to sit down, and in answer to the question replied that his object in coming over to the Russians was to help them to destroy Shamil.

"Very well, very well," said Vorontsov; "but what exactly does he wish to do? . . . Sit down, sit down!"

Hadji Murad sat down, and said that if only they would send him to the Lesghian line and would give him an army, he would guarantee to raise the whole of Daghestan and Shamil would then be unable to hold out.

"That would be excellent. . . . I'll think it over," said Vorontsov.

The interpreter translated Vorontsov's words to Hadji Murad.

Hadji Murad pondered.

"Tell the Sirdar one thing more," Hadji Murad began again, "that my family are in the hands of my enemy, and that as long as they are in the mountains I am bound and cannot serve him. Shamil would kill my wife and my mother and my children if I went openly against him. Let the prince first exchange my family for the prisoners he has, and then I will destroy Shamil or die!"

"All right, all right," said Vorontsov. "I will think it over. . . .
Now let him go to the chief of the staff and explain to him in
detail his position, intentions, and wishes."

Thus ended the first interview between Hadji Murad and
Vorontsov.

That even an Italian opera was performed at the new theater,
which was decorated in Oriental style. Vorontsov was in his
box when the striking figure of the limping Hadji Murad
wearing a turban appeared in the stalls. He came in with Loris-
Melikov, Vorontsov's aide-de-cam;, in whose charge he was
placed, and took a seat in the front row. Having sat through the
first act with Oriental Mohammedan dignity, expressing no
pleasure but only obvious indifference, he rose and looking
calmly round at the audience went out, drawing to himself
everybody's attention.

The next day was Monday and there was the usual evening
party at the Vorontsovs'. In the large brightly lighted hall a
band was playing, hidden among trees. Young women and
women not very young wearing dresses that displayed their
bare necks, arms, and breasts, turned round and round in the
embrace of men in bright uniforms. At the buffet, footmen in
red swallow-tail coats and wearing shoes and knee-breeches,
poured out champagne and served sweetmeats to the ladies.
The "Sirdar's" wife also, in spite of her age, went about half-
dressed among the visitors smiling affably, and through the
interpreter said a few amiable words to Hadji Murad who
glanced at the visitors with the same indifference he had shown
yesterday in the theater. After the hostess, other half-naked
women came up to him and all of them stood shamelessly
before him and smilingly asked him the same question: How he

liked what he saw? Vorontsov himself, wearing gold epaulets and gold shoulder-knots with his white cross and ribbon at his neck, came up and asked him the same question, evidently feeling sure, like all the others, that Hadji Murad could not help being pleased at what he saw. Hadji Murad replied to Vorontsov as he had replied to them all, that among his people nothing of the kind was done, without expressing an opinion as to whether it was good or bad that it was so.

Here at the ball Hadji Murad tried to speak to Vorontsov about buying out his family, but Vorontsov, pretending that he had not heard him, walked away, and Loris-Melikov afterwards told Hadji Murad that this was the place to talk about business.

When it struck eleven Hadji Murad, having made sure of the time by the watch the Vorontsovs had given him, asked Loris-Melikov whether he might now leave. Loris-Melikov said he might, though it would be better to stay. In spite of this Hadji Murad did not stay, but drove in the phaeton placed at his disposal to the quarters that had been assigned to him.

Leo Tolstoy

Chapter XI

On the fifth day of Hadji Murad's stay in Tiflis Loris-Melikov, the Viceroy's aide-de-camp, came to see him at the latter's command.

"My head and my hands are glad to serve the Sirdar," said Hadji Murad with his usual diplomatic expression, bowing his head and putting his hands to his chest. "Command me!" said he, looking amiably into Loris-Melikov's face.

Loris-Melikov sat down in an arm chair placed by the table and Hadji Murad sank onto a low divan opposite and, resting his hands on his knees, bowed his head and listened attentively to what the other said to him.

Loris-Melikov, who spoke Tartar fluently, told him that though the prince knew about his past life, he yet wanted to hear the whole story from himself.

Tell it me, and I will write it down and translate it into Russian and the prince will send it to the Emperor."

Hadji Murad remained silent for a while (he never interrupted anyone but always waited to see whether his interlocutor had not something more to say), then he raised his head, shook back his cap, and smiled the peculiar childlike smile that had captivated Marya Vasilevna.

"I can do that," said he, evidently flattered by the thought that his story would be read by the Emperor.

"Thou must tell me" (in Tartar nobody is addressed as "you") "everything, deliberately from the beginning," said Loris Melikov drawing a notebook from his pocket.

"I can do that, only there is much — very much — to tell! Many events have happened!" said Hadji Murad.

"If thou canst not do it all in one day thou wilt finish it another time," said Loris-Melikov.

"Shall I begin at the beginning?"

"Yes, at the very beginning . . . where thou wast born and where thou didst live."

Hadji Murad's head sank and he sat in that position for a long time. Then he took a stick that lay beside the divan, drew a little knife with an ivory gold-inlaid handle, sharp as a razor, from under his dagger, and started whittling the stick with it and speaking at the same time.

"Write: Born in Tselmess, a small aoul, 'the size of an ass's head,' as we in the mountains say," he began. "not far from it, about two cannon-shots, lies Khunzakh where the Khans lived. Our family was closely connected with them.

"My mother, when my eldest brother Osman was born, nursed the eldest Khan, Abu Nutsal Khan. Then she nursed the second son of the Khan, Umma Khan, and reared him; but Akhmet my second brother died, and when I was born and the Khansha bore Bulach Khan, my mother would not go as wet-nurse again. My father ordered her to, but she would not. She said: 'I should again kill my own son, and I will not go.' Then my father, who was passionate, struck her with a dagger and would have killed her had they not rescued her from him. So she did not give me up, and later on she composed a song . . . but I need not tell that."

"Yes, you must tell everything. It is necessary," said Loris-Melikov.

Hadji Murad grew thoughtful. He remembered how his mother had laid him to sleep beside her under a fur coat on the roof of the saklya, and he had asked her to show him the place in her side where the scar of her wound was still visible.

He repeated the song, which he remembered:

"My white bosom was pierced by the blade of bright steel,
But I laid my bright sun, my dear boy, close upon it
Till his body was bathed in the stream of my blood.
And the wound healed without aid of herbs or of grass.
As I feared not death, so my boy will ne'er fear it."

"My mother is now in Shamil's hands," he added, "and she must be rescued."

91

He remembered the fountain below the hill, when holding on to his mother's sarovary (loose Turkish trousers) he had gone with her for water. He remembered how she had shaved his head for the first time, and how the reflection of his round bluish head in the shining brass vessel that hung on the wall had astonished him. He remembered a lean dog that had licked his face. He remembered the strange smell of the lepeshki (a kind of flat cake) his mother had given him — a smell of smoke and of sour milk. He remembered how his mother had carried him in a basket on her back to visit his grandfather at the farmstead. He remembered his wrinkled grandfather with his grey hairs, and how he had hammered silver with his sinewy hands.

"Well, so my mother did not go as nurse," he said with a jerk of his head, "and the Khansha took another nurse but still remained fond of my mother, and my mother used to take us children to the Khansha's palace, and we played with her children and she was fond of us.

"There were three young Khans: Abu Nutsal Khan my brother Osman's foster-brother; Umma Khan my own sworn brother; and Bulach Khan the youngest — whom Shamil threw over the precipice. But that happened later.

"I was about sixteen when murids began to visit the aouls. They beat the stones with wooden scimitars and cried 'Mussulmans, Ghazavat!' The Chechens all went over to Muridism and the Avars began to go over too. I was then living in the palace like a brother of the Khans. I could do as I liked, and I became rich. I had horses and weapons and money. I lived for pleasure and had no care, and went on like that till the time when Kazi-Mulla, the Imam, was killed and Hamzad succeeded him. Hamzad sent envoys to the Khans to say that if they did not join the Ghazavat he would destroy Khunzakh.

"This needed consideration. The Khans feared the Russians, but were also afraid to join in the Holy War. The old Khansha sent me with her second son, Umma Khan, to Tiflis to ask the Russian Commander-in-Chief for help against Hamzad. The Commander-in-Chief at Tiflis was Baron Rosen. He did not receive either me or Umma Khan. He sent word that he would help us, but did nothing. Only his officers came riding to us and played cards with Umma Khan. They made him drunk with wine and took him to bad places, and he lost all he had to them at cards. His body was as strong as a bull's and he was as brave as a lion, but his soul was weak as water. He would have gambled away his last horses and weapons if I had not made him come away.

"After visiting Tiflis my ideas changed and I advised the old Khansha and the Khans to join the Ghazavat. . . . "

What made you change your mind?" asked Loris-Melikov. "Were you not pleased with the Russians?"

Hadji Murad paused.

"No, I was not pleased," he answered decidedly, closing his eyes. "and there was also another reason why I wished to join the Ghazavat."

"What was that?"

"Why, near Tselmess the Khan and I encountered three murids, two of whom escaped but the third one I shot with my pistol.

"He was still alive when I approached to take his weapons. He looked up at me, and said, 'Thou has killed me . . . I am happy; but thou are a Mussulman, young and strong. Join the Ghazavat! God wills it!'"

"And did you join it?"

"I did not, but it made me think," said Hadji Murad, and he went on with his tale.

"When Hamzad approached Kunzakh we sent our Elders to him to say that we would agree to join the Ghazavat if the Imam would sent a learned man to explain it to us. Hamzad had our Elders' mustaches shaved off, their nostrils pierced, and cakes hung to their noses, and in that condition he sent them back to us.

"The Elders brought word that Hamzad was ready to send a sheik to teach us the Ghazavat, but only if the Khansha sent him her youngest son as a hostage. She took him at his word and sent her youngest son, Bulach Khan. Hamzad received him well and sent to invite the two elder brothers also. He sent word that he wished to serve the Khans as his father had served their father. . . . The Khansha was a weak, stupid, and conceited woman, as all women are when they are not under control. She was afraid to send away both sons and sent only Umma Khan. I went with him. We were met by murids about a mile before we arrived and they sang and shot and caracoled around us, and when we drew near, Hamzad came out of his tent and went up to Umma Khan's stirrup and received him as a Khan. He said, 'I have not done any harm to thy family and do not wish to do any. Only do not kill me and do not prevent my bringing the people over to the Ghazavat, and I will serve you with my whole army as my father served your father! Let me live in your house and I will help you with my advice, and you shall do as you like!'

"Umma Khan was slow of speech. He did not know how to reply and remained silent. Then I said that if this was so, Let Hamzad come to Khunzakh and the Khansha and the Khans would receive him with honor. . . . but I was not allowed to finish — and here I first encountered Shamil, who was beside the Imam. He said to me, 'Thou has not been asked. . . . It was the Khan!'

"I was silent, and Hamzad led Umma Khan into his tent. Afterwards Hamzad called me and ordered me to go to Kunzakh with his envoys. I went. The envoys began persuading the Khansha to send her eldest son also to Hamzad. I saw there was treachery and told her not to send him; but a woman has as much sense in her head as an egg has hair. She ordered her son to go. Abu Nutsal Khan did not wish to. Then she said, 'I see thou are afraid!' Like a bee she knew where to sting him most painfully. Abu Nutsal Khan flushed and did not speak to her any more, but ordered his horse to be saddled. I went with him.

"Hamzad met us with even greater honor than he had shown Umma Khan. He himself rode out two rifle-shot lengths down the hill to meet us. A large party of horsemen with their banners followed him, and they too sang, shot, and caracoled.

"When we reached the camp, Hamzad led the Khan into his tent and I remained with the horses. . . .

"I was some way down the hiss when I heard shots fired in Hamzad's tent. I ran there and saw Umma Khan lying prone in a pool of blood, and Abu Nutsal was fighting the murids. One of his cheeks had been hacked off and hung down. He supported it with one hand and with the other stabbed with his dagger at all who came near him. I saw him strike down Hamzad's brother and aim a blow at another man, but then the murids fired at him and he fell."

Hadji Murad stopped and his sunburnt face flushed a dark red and his eyes became bloodshot.

"I was seized with fear and ran away."

"Really? . . . I thought thou never wast afraid," said Loris-Melikov.

"Never after that. . . . Since then I have always remembered that shame, and when I recalled it I feared nothing!"

Chapter XII

"But enough! It is time for me to pray," said Hadji Murad
drawing from an inner breast-pocket of his Circassian coat
Vorontsov's repeater watch and carefully pressing the spring.
The repeater struck twelve and a quarter. Hadji Murad listened
with his head on one side, repressing a childlike smile.

"Kunak Vorontsov's present," he said, smiling.

"It is a good watch," said Loris-Melikov. "Well then, to thou
and pray, and I will wait."

"Yakshi. Very well," said Hadji Murad and went to his
bedroom.

Left by himself, Loris-Melikov wrote down in his notebook the
chief things Hadji Murad had related, and then lighting a
cigarette began to pace up and down the room. On reaching the
door opposite the bedroom he heard animated voices speaking
rapidly in Tartar. He guessed that the speakers were Hadji
Murad's murids, and opening the door he went to them.

The room was impregnated with that special leathery acid smell peculiar to the mountaineers. On a burka spread out on the floor sat the one-eyed, red-haired Gamzalo, in a tattered greasy beshmet, plaiting a bridle. He was saying something excitedly, speaking in a hoarse voice, but when Loris-Melikov entered he immediately became silent and continued his work without paying any attention to him.

In front of Gamzalo stood the merry Khan Mahoma showing his white teeth, his black lashless eyes glittering, and saying something over and over again. The handsome Eldar, his sleeves turned up on his strong arms, was polishing the girths of a saddle suspended from a nail. Khanefi, the principal worker and manager of the household, was not there, he was cooking their dinner in the kitchen.

"What were you disputing about?" asked Loris-Melikov after greeting them.

"Why, he keeps on praising Shamil," said Khan Mahoma giving his hand to Loris-Melikov. "He says Shamil is a great man, learned, holy, and a dzhigit."

"How is it that he has left him and still praises him?"

"He has left him and still praises him," repeated Khan Mahoma, his teeth showing and his eyes glittering.

"And does he really consider him a saint?" asked Loris-Melikov.

"If he were not a saint the people would not listen to him," said Gamzalo rapidly.

"Shamil is no saint, but Mansur was!" replied Khan Mahoma. "He was a real saint. When he was Imam the people were quite different. He used to ride through the aouls and the people used to come out and kiss the him of his coat and confess their sins and vow to do no evil. Then all the people — so the old men say — lived like saints: not drinking, nor smoking, nor neglecting their prayers, and forgiving one another their sins even when blood had been spilt. If anyone then found money or anything, he tied it to a stake and set it up by the roadside. In those days God gave the people success in everything — not as now."

"In the mountains they don's smoke or drink now," said Gamzalo.

"Your Shamil is a lamorey," said Khan Mahoma, winking at Loris-Melikov. (Lamorey was a contemptuous term for a mountaineer.)

"Yes, lamorey means mountaineer," replied Gamzalo. "It is in the mountains that the eagles dwell."

"Smart fellow! Well hit!" said Khan Mahoma with a grin, pleased at his adversary's apt retort.

Seeing the silver cigarette-case in Loris Melikov's hand, Khan Mahoma asked for a cigarette, and when Loris=Melikov remarked that they were forbidden to smoke, he winded with one eye and jerking his head in the direction of Hadji Murad's bedroom replied that they could do it as long as they were not seen. He at once began smoking — not inhaling — and pouting his red lips awkwardly as he blew out the smoke.

"That is wrong!" said Gamzalo severely, and left the room. Khan Mahoma winked in his direction, and while smoking asked Loris-Melikov where he could best buy a silk beshmet and a white cap.

"Why, has thou so much money?"

"I have enough," replied Khan Mahoma with a wink.

"Ask him where he got the money," said Eldar, turning his handsome smiling face towards Loris-Melikov.

"Oh, I won it!" said Khan Mahoma quickly, and related how while walking in Tiflis the day before he had come upon a group of men — Russians and Armenians — playing at orlyanka (a kind of heads-and-tails). the stake was a large one: three gold ;pieces and much silver. Khan Mahoma at once saw what the game consisted in, and jingling the coppers he had in his pocket he went up to the players and said he would stake the whole amount.

"How couldst thou do it? Hadst thou so much?" asked Loris-Melikov.

"I had only twelve kopecks," said Khan Mahoma, grinning.

"But if thou hadst lost?"

"Why, this!" said Khan Mahoma pointing to his pistol.

"Wouldst thou have given that?"

"Give it indeed! I should have run away, and if anyone had tried to stop me I should have killed him — that's all!"

"Well, and didst thou win?"

"Aye, I won it all and went away!"

Loris-Melikov quite understood what sort of men Khan Mahoma and Eldar were. Khan Mahoma was a merry fellow, careless and ready for any spree. He did not know what to do with his superfluous vitality. He was always gay and reckless, and played with his own and other people's lives. For the sake of that sport with life he had now come over to the Russians, and for the same sport he might go back to Shamil tomorrow.

Eldar was also quite easy to understand. He was a man entirely devoted to his Murshid; calm, strong, and firm.

The red-haired Gamzalo was the only one Loris-Melikov did not understand. He saw that that man was not only loyal to Shamil but felt an insuperable aversion, contempt, repugnance, and hatred for all Russians, and Loris-Melikov could therefore not understand why he had come over to them. It occurred to him that, as some of the higher officials suspected, Hadji Murad's surrender and his tales of hatred of Shamil might be false, and that perhaps he had surrendered only to spy out the Russians' weak spots that, after escaping back to the mountains, he might be able to direct his forces accordingly. Gamzalo's whole person strengthened this suspicion.

"The others, and Hadji Murad himself, know how to hid their intentions, but this one betrays them by his open hatred," thought he.

Loris-Melikov tried to speak to him. He asked whether he did not feel dull. "No, I don't!" he growled hoarsely without stopping his work, and glancing at his questioner out of the corner of his one eye. He replied to all Loris-Melikov's other questions in a similar manner.

While Loris-Melikov was in the room Hadji Murad's fourth murid came in, the Avar Khanefi; a man with a hairy face and neck and an arched chest as rough as if it were overgrown with moss. He was strong and a hard worker, always engrossed in his duties, and like Eldar unquestioningly obedient to his master.

When he entered the room to fetch some rice, Loris-Melikov stopped him and asked where he came from and how long he had been with Hadji Murad.

"Five years," replied Khanefi. "I come from the same aoul as he. My father killed his uncle and they wished to kill me." he said calmly, looking from under his joined eyebrows straight into Loris-Melikov's face. "Then I asked them to adopt me as a brother."

"What do you mean by 'adopt as a brother'?"

"I did not shave my head nor cut my nails for two months, and then I came to them. They let me in to Patimat, his mother, and she gave me the breast and I became his brother."

Hadji Murad's voice could be heard from the next room and Eldar, immediately answering his call, promptly wiped his hands and went with large strides into the drawing room.

"He asks thee to come," said he, coming back.

Loris-Melikov gave another cigarette to the merry Khan Mahoma and went into the drawing room.

Leo Tolstoy

Chapter XIII

When Loris-Melikov entered the drawing room Hadji Murad received him with a bright face.

"Well, shall I continue?" he asked, sitting down comfortably on the divan.

"Yes, certainly," said Loris-Melikov. "I have been in to have a talk with thy henchmen. . . . One is a jolly fellow!" he added.

"Yes, Khan Mahoma is a frivolous fellow," said Hadji Murad.

"I liked the young handsome one."

"Ah, that's Eldar. He's young but firm — made of iron!"

They were silent for a while.

"So I am to on?"

"Yes, yes!"

"I told the how the Khans were killed. . . . Well, having killed them Hamzad rode into Khunzakh and took up his quarters in their palace. The Khansha was the only one of the family left alive. Hamzad sent for her. She reproached him, so he winked to his murid Aseldar, who struck her from behind and killed her."

"Why did he kill her?" asked Loris-Melikov.

"What could he do? . . . Where the forelegs have gone the hind legs must follow! He killed off the whole family. Shamil killed the youngest son — threw him over a precipice. . . .

"Then the whole of Avaria surrendered to Hamzad. But my brother and I would not surrender. We wanted his blood for the blood of the Khans. We pretended to yield, but our only thought was how to get his blood. We consulted our grandfather and decided to await the time when he would come out of his palace, and then to kill him from an ambush. Someone overheard us and told Hamzad, who sent for grandfather and said, 'Mind, if it be true that thy grandsons are planning evil against me, thou and they shall hang from one rafter. I do God's work and cannot be hindered. . . . To, and remember what I have said!'

"Our grandfather came home and told us.

"Then we decided not to wait but to do the deed on the first day of the feast in the mosque. Our comrades would not take part in it but my brother and I remained firm.

"We took two pistols each, put on our burkas, and went to the mosque. Hamzad entered the mosque with thirty murids. They

106

all had drawn swords in their hands. Aseldar, his favorite murid
(the one who had cut off Khansha's head), saw us, shouted to
us to take off our burkas, and came towards me. I had my
dagger in my hand and I killed him with it and rushed at
Hamzad; but my brother Osman had already shot him. He was
still alive and rushed at my brother dagger in hand, but I have
him a finishing blow on the head. There were thirty murids and
we were only two. They killed my brother Osman, but I kept
them at bay, leapt through the window, and escaped.

"When it was known that Hamzad had been killed all the
people rose. The murids fled and those of them who did not
flee were killed."

Hadji Murad paused, and breathed heavily.

"That was very good," he continued, "but afterwards
everything was spoilt.

"Shamil succeeded Hamzad. He sent envoys to me to say that I
should join him in attacking the Russians, and that if I refused
he would destroy Kunzakh and kill me.

"I answered that I would not join him and would not let him
come to me. . . . "

"Why didst thou not go with him?" asked Loris-Melikov.

Hadji Murad frowned and did not reply at once.

"I could not. The blood of my brother Osman and of Abu
Nutsal Khan was on his hands. I did not go to him. General
Rosen sent me an officer's commission and ordered me to

govern Avaria. All this would have been well, but that Rosen appointed as Khan of Kazi-Kumukh, first Mahomet-Murza, and afterwards Akhmet Khan, who hated me. He had been trying to get the Khansha's daughter, Sultanetta, in marriage for his son, but she would not giver her to him, and he believed me to be the cause of this. . . . Yes, Akhmet Khan hated me and sent his henchmen to kill me, but I escaped from them. Then he spoke ill of me to General Klugenau. He said that I told the Avars not to supply wood to the Russian soldiers, and he also said that I had donned a turban — this one" (Hadji Murad touched his turban) "and that this meant that I had gone over to Shamil. The general did not believe him and gave orders that I should not be touched. But when the general went to Tiflis, Akhmet Khan did as he pleased. He sent a company of soldiers to seize me, put me in chains, and tied me to a cannon.

"So they kept me six days," he continued. "On the seventh day they untied me and started to take me to Temir-Khan-Shura. Forty soldiers with loaded guns had me in charge. My hands were tied and I knew that they had orders to kill me if I tried to escape.

"As we approached Mansokha the path became narrow, and on the right was an abyss about a hundred and twenty yards deep. I went to the right — to the very edge. A soldier wanted to stop me, but I jumped down and pulled him with me. He was killed outright but I, as you see, remained alive.

"Ribs, head, arms, and leg — all were broken! I tried to crawl but grew giddy and fell asleep. I awoke wet with blood. A shepherd saw me and called some people who carried me to an aoul. My ribs and head healed, and my leg too, only it has remained short," and Hadji Murad stretched out his crooked leg. "It still serves me, however, and that is well," said he.

"The people heard the news and began coming to me. I recovered and went to Tselmess. The Avars again called on me to rule over them," he went on, with tranquil, confident pride, "and I agreed."

He rose quickly and taking a portfolio out of a saddlebag, drew out two discolored letters and handed one of them to Loris-Melikov. They were from General Klugenau. Loris-Melikov read the first letter, which was as follows:

"Lieutenant Hadji Murad, thou has served under me and I was satisfied with thee and considered thee a good man.

"Recently Akhmet Khan informed me that thou are a traitor, that thou has donned a turban and has intercourse with Shamil, and that thou has taught the people to disobey the Russian Government. I ordered thee to be arrested and brought before me but thou fledst. I do not know whether this is for thy good or not, as I do not know whether thou art guilty or not.

"Now hear me. If thy conscience is pure, if thou are not guilty in anything towards the great Tsar, come to me, fear no one. I am thy defender. The Khan can do nothing to thee, he is himself under my command, so thou has nothing to fear."

Klugenau added that he always kept his word and was just, and he again exhorted Hadji Murad to appear before him.

When Loris-Melikov had read this letter Hadji Murad, before handing him the second one, told him what he had written in reply to the first.

"I wrote that I wore a turban not for Shamil's sake but for my soul's salvation; that I neither wished nor could go over to Shamil, because he had cause the death of my father, my brothers, and my relations; but that I could not join the Russians because I had been dishonored by them. (In Khunzakh, a scoundrel had spat on me while I was bound, and I could not join your people until that man was killed.) But above all I feared that liar, Akhmet Khan.

"Then the general sent me this letter," said Hadji Murad, handing Loris-Melikov the other discolored paper.

"Thou has answered my first letter and I thank thee," read Loris-Melikov. "Thou writest that thou are not afraid to return but that the insult done thee by a certain giarou prevents it, but I assure thee that the Russian law is just and that thou shalt see him who dared to offend thee punished before thine eyes. I have already given orders to investigate the matter.

"Hear me, Hadji Murad! I have a right to be displeased with thee for not trusting me and my honor, but I forgive thee, for I know how suspicious mountaineers are in general. If thy conscience is pure, if thou hast put on a turban only for they soul's salvation, then thou art right and mayst look me and the Russian Government boldly in the eye. He who dishonored thee shall, I assure thee, be punished and thy property shall be restored to thee, and thou shalt see and know what Russian law is. Moreover we Russians look at things differently, and thou

110

hast not sunk in our eyes because some scoundrel has dishonored thee.

"I myself have consented to the Chimrints wearing turbans, and I regard their actions in the right light, and therefore I repeat that thou hast nothing to fear. Come to me with the man by whom I am sending thee this letter. He is faithful to me and is not the slave of thy enemies, but is the friend of a man who enjoys the special favor of the Government."

Further on Klugenau again tried to persuade Hadji Murad to come over to him.

"I did not believe him," said Hadji Murad when Loris-Melikov had finished reading, "and did not go to Klugenau. The chief thing for me was to revenge myself on Akhmet Khan, and that I could not do through the Russians. Then Akhmet Khan surrounded Tselmess and wanted to take me or kill me. I had too few men and could not drive him off, and just then came an envoy with a letter from Shamil promising to help me to defeat and kill Akhmet Khan and making me ruler over the whole of Avaria. I considered the matter for a long time and then went over to Shamil, and from that time I have fought the Russians continually."

Here Hadji Murad related all his military exploits, of which there were very many and some of which were already familiar to Loris-Melikov. all his campaigns and raids had been remarkable for the extraordinary rapidity of his movements and the boldness of his attacks, which were always crowned with success.

"There never was any friendship between me and Shamil," said Hadji Murad at the end of his story, "but he feared me and needed me. But it so happened that I was asked who should be Imam after Shamil, and I replied: 'He will be Imam whose sword is sharpest!'

"This was told to Shamil and he wanted to get rid of me. He sent me into Tabasaran. I went, and captured a thousand sheep and three hundred horses, but he said I had not done the right thing and dismissed me from being Naib, and ordered me to send him all the money. I sent him a thousand gold pieces. He sent his murids and they took from me all my property. He demanded that I should go to him, but I knew he wanted to kill me and I did not go. Then he sent to take me. I resisted and went over to Vorontsov. Only I did not take my family. My mother, my wives, and my son are in his hands. Tell the Sirdar that as long as my family is in Shamil's power I can do nothing."

"I will tell him," said Loris-Melikov.

"Take pains, try hard!. . . . What is mine is thine, only help me with the Prince. I am tied up and the end of the rope is in Shamil's hands," said Hadji Murad concluding his story.

Chapter XIV

On the 20th of December Vorontsov wrote to Chernyshov, the Minister of War. The letter was in French:

"I did not write to you by the last post, dear Prince, as I wished first to decide what we should do with Hadji Murad, and for the last two or three days I have not been feeling quite well.

"In my last letter I informed you of Hadji Murad's arrival here. He reached Tiflis on the 8th, and next day I made his acquaintance, and during the following seven or eight days have spoken to him and considered what use we can make of him in the future, and especially what we are to do with him at present, for he is much concerned about the fate of his family, and with every appearance of perfect frankness says that while they are in Shamil's hands he is paralysed and cannot render us any service or show his gratitude for the friendly reception and forgiveness we have extended to him.

"His uncertainty about those dear to him makes him restless, and the persons I have appointed to live with him assure me that he does not sleep at night, eats hardly anything, prays

113

continually, and asks only to be allowed to ride out accompanied by several Cossacks — the sole recreation and exercise possible for him and made necessary to him by life-long habit. Every day he comes to me to know whether I have any news of his family, and to ask me to have all the prisoners in our hands collected and offered to Shamil in exchange for them. He would also give a little money. There are people who would let him have some for the purpose. He keeps repeating to me: 'Save my family and then give me a chance to serve thee' (preferably, in his opinion, on the Lesghian line), 'and if within a month I do not render you great service, punish me as you think fit.' I reply that to me all this appears very just, and that many among us would even not trust him so long as his family remain in the mountains and are not in our hands as hostages, and that I will do everything possible to collect the prisoners on our frontier, that I have no power under our laws to give him money for the ransom of his family in addition to the sum he may himself be able to raise, but that I may perhaps find some other means of helping him. After that I told him frankly that in my opinion Shamil would not in any case give up the family, and that Shamil might tell him so straight out and promise him a full pardon and his former posts, and might threaten if Hadji Murad did not return, to kill his mother, his wives, and his six children. I asked him whether he could say frankly what he would do if he received such an announcement from Shamil. He lifted his eyes and arms to heaven, and said that everything is in God's hands, but that he would never surrender to his foe, for he is certain Shamil would not forgive him and he would therefore not have long to live. As to the destruction of his family, he did not think Shamil would act so rashly: firstly, to avoid making him a yet more desperate and dangerous foe, and secondly, because there were many people, and even very influential people, in Daghestan, who would dissuade Shamil from such a course. Finally, he repeated several times that whatever God might decree for him in the future, he was at present interested in nothing but his family's ransom, and he implored me in God's name to help him and allow him to return to the neighborhood of the Chechnya, where he could, with the help and consent of our commanders, have some intercourse with his family and regular news of their condition and of the best means to liberate them. He said that many people, and even some Naibs in that part of the enemy's territory, were more or less attached to him and that among the whole of the population already subjugated by Russia or neutral it would be easy with our help to establish relations very useful for the attainment of the aim which gives him no peace day or night, and the attainment of which would set him at ease and make it possible for him to act for our good and win our confidence.

"He asks to be sent back to Grozny with a convoy of twenty or thirty picked Cossacks who would serve him as a protection against foes and us as a guarantee of his good faith.

"You will understand, dear Prince, that I have been much perplexed by all this, for do what I will a great responsibility rests on me. It would be in the highest degree rash to trust him entirely, yet in order to deprive him of all means of escape we should have to lock him up, and in my opinion that would be both unjust and impolitic. A measure of that kind, the news of which would soon spread over the whole of Daghestan, would do us great harm by keeping back those who are now inclined more or less openly to oppose Shamil (and there are many such), and who are keenly watching to see how we treat the Imam's bravest and most adventurous officer now that he has found himself obliged to place himself in our hands. If we treat

115

Hadji Murad as a prisoner all the good effect of the situation will be lost. Therefore I think that I could not act otherwise than as I have done, though at the same time I feel that I may be accused of having made a great mistake if Hadji Murad should take it into his head to escape again. In the service, and especially in a complicated situation such as this, it is difficult, not to say impossible, to follow any one straight path without risking mistakes and without accepting responsibility, but once a path seems to be the right one I must follow it, happen what may.

"I beg of you, dear Prince, to submit this to his Majesty the Emperor for his consideration; and I shall be happy if it pleases our most august monarch to approve my action.

"All that I have written above I have also written to Generals Zavodovsky and Kozlovsky, to guide the latter when communicating direct with Hadji Murad whom I have warned not to act or go anywhere without Kozlovsky's consent. I also told him that it would be all the better of us if he rode out with our convoy, as otherwise Shamil might spread a rumor that we were keeping him prisoner, but at the same time I made him promise never to go to Vozdvizhensk, because my son, to whom he first surrendered and whom he looks upon as his kunak (friend), is not the commander of that place and some unpleasant misunderstanding might easily arise. In any case Vozdvizhensk lies too near a thickly populated hostile settlement, which for the intercourse with his friends which he desires, Grozny is in all respects suitable.

"Besides the twenty chosen Cossacks who at his own request are to keep close to him, I am also sending Captain Loris-Melikov — a worthy, excellent, and highly intelligence officer who speaks Tartar, and knows Hadji Murad well and apparently enjoys his full confidence. During the ten days that Hadji Murad has spent here, he has, however, lived in the same house with Lieutenant-Colonel Prince Tarkhanov, who is in command of the shoushin District and is here on business connected with the service. He is a truly worthy man whom I trust entirely. He also has won Hadji Murad's confidence, and through him alone — as he speaks Tartar perfectly — we have discussed the most delicate and secret matters. I have consulted Tarkhanov about Hadji Murad, and he fully agrees with me that it was necessary either to act as I have done, or to put Hadji Murad in prison and guard him in the strictest manner (for if we once treat him badly he will not be easy to hold), or else to remove him from the country altogether. But these two last measures would not only destroy all the advantage accruing to us from Hadji Murad's quarrel with Shamil, but would inevitably check any growth of the present insubordination, and possible future revolt, of the people against Shamil's power. Prince Tarkhanov tells me he himself has no doubt of Hadji Murad's truthfulness, and that Hadji Murad is convinced that Shamil will never forgive him but would have him executed in spite of any promise of forgiveness. The only thing Tarkhanov has noticed in his intercourse with Hadji Murad that might cause any anxiety, is his attachment to his religion. Tarkhanov does not deny that Shamil might influence Hadji Murad from that side. But as I have already said, he will never persuade Hadji Murad that he will not take his life sooner or later should the latter return to him.

"This, dear Prince, is all I have to tell you about this episode in our affairs here."

117

Leo Tolstoy

Chapter XV

The report was dispatched from Tiflis on the 24th of December 1851, and on New Year's Eve a courier, having overdriven a dozen horses and beaten a dozen drivers till they bled, delivered it to Prince Chernyshov who at that time was Minister of War; and on the 1st of January 1852 Chernyshov took Vorontsov's report, among other papers, to the Emperor Nicholas.

Chernyshov disliked Vorontsov because of the general respect in which the latter was held and because of his immense wealth, and also because Vorontsov was a real aristocrat while Chernyshov, after all, was a parvenu, but especially because the Emperor was particularly well disposed towards Vorontsov. Therefore at every opportunity Chernyshov tried to injure Vorontsov.

When he had last presented the report about Caucasian affairs he had succeeded in arousing Nicholas's displeasure against Vorontsov because — through the carelessness of those in command — almost the whole of a small Caucasian detachment had been destroyed by the mountaineers. He now

intended to present the steps taken by Vorontsov in relation to
Hadji Murad in an unfavorable light. He wished to suggest to
the Emperor that Vorontsov always protected and even
indulged the natives to the detriment of the Russians, and that
he had acted unwisely in allowing Hadji Murad to remain in
the Caucasus for there was every reason to suspect that he had
only come over to spy on our means of defense, and that it
would therefore be better to transport him to Central Russia
and make use of him only after his family had been rescued
from the mountaineers and it had become possible to convince
ourselves of his loyalty.

Chernyshov's plan did not succeed merely because on that
New Year's Day Nicholas was in particularly bad spirits, and
out of perversity would not have accepted any suggestion
whatever from anyone, least of all from Chernyshov whom he
only tolerated — regarding him as indispensable for the time
being but looking upon him as a blackguard, for Nicholas knew
of his endeavors at the trial of the Decembrists to secure the
conviction of Zachary Chernyshov, and of his attempt to obtain
Zachary's property for himself. So thanks to Nicholas's ill
temper Hadji Murad remained in the Caucasus, and his
circumstances were not changed as they might have been had
Chernyshov presented his report at another time.

* * *

It was half-past nine o'clock when through the mist of the cold
morning (the thermometer showed 13 degrees below zero
Fahrenheit) Chernyshov's fat, bearded coachman, sitting on the
box of a small sledge (like the one Nicholas drove about in)
with a sharp-angled, cushion-shaped azure velvet cap on his
head, drew up at the entrance of the Winter Palace and gave a

friendly nod to his chum, Prince Dolgoruky's coachman —
who having brought his master to the palace had himself long
been waiting outside, in his big coat with the thickly wadded
skirts, sitting on the reins and rubbing his numbed hands
together. Chernyshov had on a long cloak with a large cap and
a fluffy collar of silver beaver, and a regulation three-cornered
had with cocks' feathers. He threw back the bearskin apron of
the sledge and carefully disengaged his chilled feet, on which
he had no over-shoes (he prided himself on never wearing
any). Clanking his spurs with an air of bravado he ascended the
carpeted steps and passed through the hall door which was
respectfully opened for him by the porter, and entered the hall.
Having thrown off his cloak which an old Court lackey hurried
forward to take, he went to a mirror and carefully removed the
hat from his curled wig. Looking at himself in the mirror, he
arranged the hair on his temples and the tuft above his forehead
with an accustomed movement of his old hands, and adjusted
his cross, the shoulder-knots of his uniform, and his large-
initialled epaulets, and then went up the gently ascending
carpeted stairs, his not very reliable old legs feebly mounting
the shallow steps. Passing the Court lackeys in gala livery who
stood obsequiously bowing, Chernyshov entered the waiting-
room. He was respectfully met by a newly appointed aide-de-
camp of the Emperor's in a shining new uniform with epaulets
and shoulder-knots, whose face was still fresh and rosy and
who had a small black mustache, and the hair on his temples
brushed towards his eyes in the same way as the Emperor.

Prince Vasili Dolgoruky, Assistant-Minister of War, with an
expression of ennui on his dull face — which was ornamented
with similar whiskers, mustaches, and temple tufts brushed
forward like Nicholas's — greeted him.

"L'empereur?" said Chernyshov, addressing the aide-de-camp and looking inquiringly towards the door leading to the cabinet.

"Sa majeste vient de rentrer," replied the aide-de-camp, evidently enjoying the sound of his own voice, and stepping so softly and steadily that had a tumbler of water been placed on his head none of it would have been spilt, he approached the door and disappeared, his whole body evincing reverence for the spot he was about to visit.

Dolgoruky meanwhile opened his portfolio to see that it contained the necessary papers, while Chernyshov, frowning, paced up and down to restore the circulation in his numbed feet, and thought over what he was about to report to the Emperor. He was near the door of the cabinet when it opened again and the aide- de-camp, even more radiant and respectful than before, came out and with a gesture invited the minister and his assistant to enter.

The Winter Palace had been rebuilt after a fire some considerable time before this, but Nicholas was still occupying rooms in the upper story. The cabinet in which he received the reports of his ministers and other high officials was a very lofty apartment with four large windows. A big portrait of the Emperor Alexander I hung on the front side of the room. Two bureaux stood between the windows, and several chairs were ranged along the walls. IN the middle of the room was an enormous writing table and an arm chair before it for Nicholas, and other chairs for those to whom he gave audience.

Nicholas sat at the table in a black coat with shoulder-straps but no epaulets, his enormous body — with his overgrown stomach tightly laced in — was thrown back, and he gazed at the newcomers with fixed, lifeless eyes. His long pale face, with its enormous receding forehead between the tufts of hair which were brushed forward and skillfully joined to the wig that covered his bald patch, was specially cold and stony that day. His eyes, always dim, looked duller than usual, the compressed lips under his upturned mustaches, the high collar which supported his chin, and his fat freshly shaven cheeks on which symmetrical sausage-shaped bits of whiskers had been left, gave his face a dissatisfied and even irate expression. His bad mood was caused by fatigue, due to the fact that he had been to a masquerade the night before, and while walking about as was his wont in his Horse Guards' uniform with a bird on the helmet, among the public which crowded round and timidly made way for his enormous, self-assured figure, he had again met the mask who at the previous masquerade had aroused his senile sensuality by her whiteness, her beautiful figure, and her tender voice. At that former masquerade she had disappeared after promising to meet him at the next one.

At yesterday's masquerade she had come up to him, and this time he had not let her go, but had led her to the box specially kept ready for that purpose, where he could be alone with her. Having arrived in silence at the door of the box Nicholas looked round to find the attendant, but he was not there. He frowned and pushed the door open himself, letting the lady enter first.

"Il y a quelq'un!" said the mask, stopping short.

And the box actually was occupied. On the small velvet-covered sofa, close together, sat an Uhlan officer and a pretty, fair curly-haired young woman in a domino, who had removed her mask. On catching sight of the angry figure of Nicholas

123

drawn up to its full height, she quickly replaced her mask, but the Uhlan officer, rigid with fear, gazed at Nicholas with fixed eyes without rising from the sofa.

Used as he was to the terror he inspired in others, that terror always pleased Nicholas, and by way of contrast he sometimes liked to astound those plunged in terror by addressing kindly words to them. He did so on this occasion.

"Well, friend!" said he to the officer, "You are younger than I and might give up your place to me."

The officer jumped to his feet, and growing first pale and then red and bending almost double, he followed his partner silently out of the box, leaving Nicholas alone with his lady.

She proved to be a pretty, twenty-year-old virgin, the daughter of a Swedish governess. She told Nicholas how when quite a child she had fallen in love with him from his portraits; how she adored him and had made up her mind to attract his attention at any cost. Now she had succeeded and wanted nothing more — so she said.

The girl was taken to the place where Nicholas usually had rendezvous with women, and there he spent more than an hour with her.

When he returned to his room that night and lay on the hard narrow bed about which he prided himself, and covered himself with the cloak which he considered to be (and spoke of as being) as famous as Napoleon's hat, it was a long time before he could fall asleep. He thought now of the frightened and elated expression on that girl's fair face, and now of the full, powerful shoulders of his established mistress, Nelidova, and he compared the two. That profligacy in a married man was a bad thing did not once enter his head, and he would have been greatly surprised had anyone censured him for it. Yet though convinced that he had acted rightly, some kind of unpleasant after-taste remained, and to stifle that feeling he dwelt on a thought that always tranquilized him — the thought of his own greatness.

Though he had fallen asleep so late, he rose before eight, and after attending to his toilet in the usual way — rubbing his big well-fed body all over with ice — and saying his prayers (repeating those he had been used to from childhood — the prayer to the Virgin, the apostles' Creed, and the Lord's Prayer, without attaching any kind of meaning to the words he uttered), he went out through the smaller portico of the palace onto the embankment in his military cloak and cap.

On the embankment he met a student in the uniform of the School of Jurisprudence, who was as enormous as himself. On recognizing the uniform of that school, which he disliked for its freedom of thought, Nicholas frowned, but the stature of the student and the painstaking manner in which he drew himself up and saluted, ostentatiously sticking out his elbow, mollified his displeasure.

"Your name?" said he.

"Polosatov, your Imperial Majesty."

". . . fine fellow!"

The student continued to stand with his hand lifted to his hat.

Nicholas stopped.

"Do you wish to enter the army?"

"Not at all, your Imperial Majesty."

"Blockhead!" And Nicholas turned away and continued his walk, and began uttering aloud the first words that came into his head.

"Kopervine . . . Kopervine — " he repeated several times (it was the name of yesterday's girl). "Horrid . . . horrid — " He did not think of what he was saying, but stifled his feelings by listening to the words.

"Yes, what would Russia be without me?" said he, feeling his former dissatisfaction returning. "What would — not Russia alone but Europe be, without me?" and calling to mind the weakness and stupidity of his brother-in-law the King of Prussia, he shook his head.

As he was returning to the small portico, he saw the carriage of Helena Pavlovna, with a red-liveried footman, approaching the Saltykov entrance of the palace.

Helena Pavlovna was to him the personification of that futile class of people who discussed not merely science and poetry, but even the ways of governing men: imagining that they could govern themselves better than he, Nicholas, governed them! He knew that however much he crushed such people they reappeared again and again, and he recalled his brother, Michael Pavlovich, who had died not long before. A feeling of sadness and vexation came over him and with a dark frown he again began whispering the first words that came into his head, which he only ceased doing when he re-entered the palace.

On reaching his apartments he smoothed his whiskers and the hair on his temples and the wig on his bald patch, and twisted his mustaches upwards in front of the mirror, and then went straight to the cabinet in which he received reports.

He first received Chernyshov, who at once saw by his face, and especially by his eyes, that Nicholas was in a particularly bad humor that day, and knowing about the adventure of the night before he understood the cause. Having coldly greeted him and invited him to sit down, Nicholas fixed on him a lifeless gaze. The first matter Chernyshov reported upon was a case of embezzlement by commissariat officials which had just been discovered; the next was the movement of troops on the Prussian frontier; then came a list of rewards to be given at the New Year to some people omitted from a former list; then Vorontsov's report about Hadji Murad; and lastly some unpleasant business concerning an attempt by a student of the Academy of Medicine on the life of a professor.

Nicholas heard the report of the embezzlement silently with compressed lips, his large white hand — with one ring on the fourth finger — stroking some sheets of paper, and his eyes steadily fixed on Chernyshov's forehead and on the tuft of hair above it.

Nicholas was convinced that everybody stole. He knew he would have to punish the commissariat officials now, and decided to send them all to serve in the ranks, but he also knew that this would not prevent those who succeeded them from acting in the same way. It was a characteristic of officials to steal, but it was his duty to punish them for doing so, and tired as he was of that duty he conscientiously performed it.

"It seems there is only one honest man in Russia!" said he.

Chernyshov at once understood that this one honest man was Nicholas himself, and smiled approvingly.

"It looks like it, your Imperial Majesty," said he.

"Leave it — I will give a decision," said Nicholas, taking the document and putting it on the left side of the table.

Then Chernyshov reported the rewards to be given and about moving the army on the Prussian frontier.

Nicholas looked over the list and struck out some names, and then briefly and firmly gave orders to move two divisions to the Prussian frontier. He could not forgive the King of Prussia for granting a Constitution to his people after the events of 1848, and therefore while expressing most friendly feelings to his brother-in-law in letters and conversation, he considered it necessary to keep an army near the frontier in case of need. He might want to use these troops to defend his brother-in-law's throne if the people of Prussia rebelled (Nicholas saw a readiness for rebellion everywhere) as he had used troops to suppress the rising in Hungary a few years previously. they were also of use to give more weight and influence to such advice as he gave to the King of Prussia.

"Yes — what would Russia be like now if it were not for me?" he again thought.

"Well, what else is there?" said he.

"A courier from the Caucasus," said Chernyshov, and he reported what Vorontsov had written about Hadji Murad's surrender.

"Well, well!" said Nicholas. "It's a good beginning!"

"Evidently the plan devised by your Majesty begins to bear fruit," said Chernyshov.

this approval of his strategic talents was particularly pleasant to Nicholas because, though he prided himself upon them, at the bottom of his heart he knew that they did not really exist, and he now desired to hear more detailed praise of himself.

"How do you mean?" he asked.

"I mean that if your Majesty's plans had been adopted before, and we had moved forward slowly and steadily, cutting down forests and destroying the supplies of food, the Caucasus would have been subjugated long ago. I attribute Hadji Murad's surrender entirely to his having come to the conclusion that they can hold out no longer."

"True," said Nicholas.

Although the plan of a gradual advance into the enemy's territory by means of felling forests and destroying the food supplies was Ermolov's and Velyaminov's plan, and was quite contrary to Nicholas's own plan of seizing Shamil's place of residence and destroying that nest of robbers — which was the plan on which the dargo expedition in 1845 (that cost so many lives) had been undertaken — Nicholas nevertheless attributed to himself also the plan of a slow advance and a systematic felling of forests and devastation of the country. It would seem that to believe the plan of a slow movement by felling forests and destroying food supplies to have been his own would have necessitated hiding the fact that he had insisted on quite contrary operations in 1845. But he did not hide it and was proud of the plan of the 1845 expedition as well as of the plan of a slow advance — though the two were obviously contrary to one another. Continual brazen flattery from everybody round him in the teeth of obvious facts had brought him to such a state that he no longer saw his own inconsistencies or measured his actions and words by reality, logic, or even simple common sense; but was quite convinced that all his orders, however senseless, unjust, and mutually contradictory they might be, became reasonable, just, and mutually accordant simply because he gave them. His decision in the case next reported to him — that of the student of the Academy of Medicine — was of the that senseless kind.

The case was as follows: A young man who had twice failed in his examinations was being examined a third time, and when the examiner again would not pass him, the young man whose nerves were deranged, considering this to be an injustice, seized a pen-knife from the table in a paroxysm of fury, and rushing at the professor inflicted on him several trifling wounds.

"What's his name?" asked Nicholas.

"Bzhezovski."

"A Pole?"

"Of Polish descent and a roman Catholic," answered
Chernyshov.

Nicholas frowned. He had done much evil to the Poles. To
justify that evil he had to feel certain that all Poles were
rascals, and he considered them to be such and hated them in
proportion to the evil he had done them.

"Wait a little," he said, closing his eyes and bowing his head.

Chernyshov, having more than once heard Nicholas say so,
knew that when the Emperor had to take a decision it was only
necessary for him to concentrate his attention for a few
moments and the spirit moved him, and the best possible
decision presented itself as though an inner voice had told him
what to do. He was now thinking how most fully to satisfy the
feeling of hatred against the Poles which this incident had
stirred up within him, and the inner voice suggested the
following decision. He took the report and in his large
handwriting wrote on its margin with three orthographical
mistakes:

"Diserves deth, but, thank God, we have no capitle
punishment, and it is not for me to introduce it. Make him fun
the gauntlet of a thousand men twelve times. — Nicholas."

He signed, adding his unnaturally huge flourish.

Nicholas knew that twelve thousand strokes with the regulation
rods were not only certain death with torture, but were a
superfluous cruelty, for five thousand strokes were sufficient to

kill the strongest man. But it pleased him to be ruthlessly cruel and it also pleased him to think that we have abolished capital punishment in Russia.

Having written his decision about the student, he pushed it across to Chernyshov.

"There," he said, "read it."

Chernyshov read it, and bowed his head as a sign of respectful amazement at the wisdom of the decision.

"Yes, and let all the students be present on the drill-ground at the punishment," added Nicholas.

"It will do them good! I will abolish this revolutionary spirit and will tear it up by the roots!" he thought.

"It shall be done," replied Chernyshov; and after a short pause he straightened the tuft on his forehead and returned to the Caucasian report.

"What do you command me to write in reply to Prince Vorontsov's dispatch?"

"To keep firmly to my system of destroying the dwellings and food supplies in Chechnya and to harass them by raids." answered Nicholas.

"And what are your Majesty's commands with reference to Hadji Murad?" asked Chernyshov.

"Well, Vorontsov writes that he wants to make use of him in the Caucasus."

"Is it not dangerous?" said Chernyshov, avoiding Nicholas's gaze. "Prince Vorontsov is too confiding, I am afraid."

"And you — what do you think?" asked Nicholas sharply, detecting Chernyshov's intention of presenting Vorontsov's decision in an unfavorable light.

"Well, I should have thought it would be safer to deport him to Central Russia."

"You would have thought!" said Nicholas ironically. "But I don't think so, and agree with Vorontsov. Write to him accordingly."

"It shall be done," said Chernyshov, rising and bowing himself out.

Dolgoruky also bowed himself out, having during the whole audience only uttered a few words (in reply to a question from Nicholas) about the movement of the army.

After Chernyshov, Nicholas received Bibikov, General-Governor of the Western Provinces. Having expressed his approval of the measures taken by Bibikov against the mutinous peasants who did not wish to accept the orthodox Faith, he ordered him to have all those who did not submit tried by court-martial. that was equivalent to sentencing them to run the gauntlet. He also ordered the editor of a newspaper to be sent to serve in the ranks of the army for publishing

information about the transfer of several thousand State
peasants to the imperial estates.

"I do this because I consider it necessary," said Nicholas, "and
I will not allow it to be discussed."

Bibikov saw the cruelty of the order concerning the Uniate
peasants and the injustice of transferring State peasants (the
only free peasants in Russia in those days) to the Crown, which
meant making them serfs of the Imperial family. But it was
impossible to express dissent. Not to agree with Nicholas's
decisions would have meant the loss of that brilliant position
which it had cost Bibikov forty years to attain and which he
now enjoyed; and he therefore submissively bowed his dark
head (already touched with grey) to indicate his submission
and his readiness to fulfil the cruel, insensate, and dishonest
supreme will.

Having dismissed Bibikov, Nicholas stretched himself, with a
sense of duty well fulfilled, glanced at the clock, and went to
get ready to go out. Having put on a uniform with epaulets,
orders, and a ribbon, he went out into the reception hall where
more than a hundred persons — men in uniforms and women
in elegant low-necked dresses, all standing in the places
assigned to them — awaited his arrival with agitation.

He came out to them with a lifeless look in his eyes, his chest
expanded, his stomach bulging out above and below its
bandages, and feeling everybody's gaze tremulously and
obsequiously fixed upon him he assumed an even more
triumphant air. When his eyes met those of people he knew,
remembering who was who, he stopped and addressed a few
words to them sometimes in Russian and sometimes in French,

and transfixing them with his cold glassy eye listened to what they said.

Having received all the New year congratulations he passed on to church, where God, through His servants the priests, greeted and praised Nicholas just as worldly people did; and weary as he was of these greetings and praises Nicholas duly accepted them. All this was as it should be, because the welfare and happiness of the whole world depended on him, and wearied though he was he would still not refuse the universe his assistance.

When at the end of the service the magnificently arrayed deacon, his long hair crimped and carefully combed, began the chant "Many Years," which was heartily caught up by the splendid choir, Nicholas looked round and noticed Nelidova, with her fine shoulders, standing by a window, and he decided the comparison with yesterday's girl in her favor.

After Mass he went to the empress and spent a few minutes in the bosom of his family, joking with the children and his wife. then passing through the Hermitage, he visited the Minister of the Court, Volkonski, and among other things ordered him to pay out of a special fund a yearly pension to the mother of yesterday's girl. From there he went for his customary drive.

Dinner that day was served in the Pompeian Hall. Besides the younger sons of Nicholas and Michael there were also invited Baron Lieven, Count Rzhevski, Dolgoruky, the Prussian Ambassador, and the King of Prussia's aide-de-camp.

While waiting for the appearance of the Emperor and Empress an interesting conversation took place between Baron Lieven and the Prussian Ambassador concerning the disquieting news from Poland.

"La Pologne et le Caucases, ce sont les deux cauteres de la Russie," said Lieven. "Il nous faut dent mille hommes a peu pres, dans chcun de ces deux pays."

The Ambassador expressed a fictitious surprise that it should be so.

"Vous dites, la Pologne — " began the Ambassador.

"Oh, oui, c'etait un coup de maitre de Metternich de nous en avoir laisse l'embarras. . . . "

At this point the Empress, with her trembling head and fixed smile, entered followed by Nicholas.

At dinner Nicholas spoke of Hadji Murad's surrender and said that the war in the Caucasus must now soon come to an end in consequence of the measures he was taking to limit the scope of the mountaineers by felling their forests and by his system of erecting a series of small forts.

The Ambassador, having exchanged a rapid glance with the aide-de-camp — to whom he had only that morning spoken about Nicholas's unfortunate weakness for considering himself a great strategist — warmly praised this plan which once more demonstrated Nicholas's great strategic ability.

After dinner Nicholas drove to the ballet where hundreds of women marched round in tights and scanty clothing. One of the specially attracted him, and he had the German ballet-master sent for and gave orders that a diamond ring should be presented to her.

The next day when Chernyshov came with his report, Nicholas again confirmed his order to Vorontsov — that now that Hadji Murad had surrendered, the Chechens should be more actively harassed than ever and the cordon round them tightened.

Chernyshov wrote in that sense to Vorontsov; and another courier, overdriving more horses and bruising the faces of more drivers, galloped to Tiflis.

Leo Tolstoy

Chapter XVI

In obedience to this command of Nicholas a raid was immediately made in Chechnya that same month, January 1852.

The detachment ordered for the raid consisted of four infantry battalions, two companies of Cossacks, and eight guns. The column marched along the road; and on both sides of it in a continuous line, now mounting, now descending, marched Fagers in high boots, sheepskin coats, and tall caps, with rifles on their shoulders and cartridges in their belts.

As usual when marching through a hostile country, silence was observed as far as possible. Only occasionally the guns jingled jolting across a ditch, or an artillery horse snorted or neighed, not understanding that silence was ordered, or an angry commander shouted in a hoarse subdued voice to his subordinates that the line was spreading out too much or marching too near or too far from the column. Only once was the silence broken, when from a bramble patch between the line and the column a gazelle with a white breast and grey back jumped out followed by a buck of the same color with small

139

backward-curving horns. Doubling up their forelegs at each big bound they took, the beautiful timid creatures came so close to the column that some of the soldiers rushed after them laughing and shouting, intending to bayonet them, but the gazelles turned back, slipped through the line of Fagers, and pursued by a few horsemen and the company's dogs, fled like birds to the mountains.

It was still winter, but towards noon, when the column (which had started early in the morning) had gone three miles, the sun had risen high enough and was powerful enough to make the men quite hot, and its rays were so bright that it was painful to look at the shining steel of the bayonets or at the reflections — like little suns — on the brass of the cannons.

The clear and rapid stream the detachment had just crossed lay behind, and in front were tilled fields and meadows in shallow valleys. Farther in front were the dark mysterious forest-clad hills with craigs rising beyond them, and farther still on the lofty horizon were the ever-beautiful ever-changing snowy peaks that played with the light like diamonds.

At the head of the 5th Company, Butler, a tall handsome officer who had recently exchanged from the Guards, marched along in a black coat and tall cap, shouldering his sword. He was filled with a buoyant sense of the joy of living, the danger of death, a wish for action, and the consciousness of being part of an immense whole directed by a single will. This was his second time of going into action and he thought how in a moment they would be fired at, and he would not only not stoop when the shells flew overhead, or heed the whistle of the bullets, but would carry his head even more erect than before and would look round at his comrades and the soldiers with smiling eyes, and begin to talk in a perfectly calm voice about quite other matters.

The detachment turned off the good road onto a little-used one that crossed a stubbly maize field, ant they were drawing near the forest when, with an ominous whistle, a shell flew past amid the baggage wagons — they could not see whence — and tore up the ground in the field by the roadside.

"It's beginning," said Butler with a bright smile to a comrade who was walking beside him.

And so it was. After the shell a thick crowd of mounted Chechens appeared with their banners from under the shelter of the forest. In the midst of the crowd could be seen a large green banner, and an old and very far-sighted sergeant-major informed the short-sighted Butler that Shamil himself must be there. The horsemen came down the hiss and appeared to the right, at the highest part of the valley nearest the detachment, and began to descend. A little general in a thick black coat and tall cap rode up to Butler's company on his ambler, and ordered him to the right to encounter the descending horsemen. Butler quickly led his company in the direction indicated, but before he reached the valley he heard two cannon shots behind him. He looked round: two clouds of grey smoke had risen above two cannon and were spreading along the valley. The mountaineers' horsemen — who had evidently not expected to meet artillery — retired. Butler's company began firing at them and the whole ravine was filled with the smoke of powder. Only higher up above the ravine could the mountaineers be seen hurriedly retreating, though still firing back at the Cossacks who pursued them. The company followed the mountaineers farther, and on the slope of a second ravine came in view of an aoul.

Following the Cossacks, Butler and his company entered the aoul at a run, to find it deserted. The soldiers were ordered to burn the corn and the hay as well as the saklyas, and the whole aoul was soon filled with pungent smoke amid which the soldiers rushed about dragging out of the saklyas what they could find, and above all catching and shooting the fowls the mountaineers had not been able to take away with them.

The officers sat down at some distance beyond the smoke, and lunched and drank. The sergeant-major brought them some honeycombs on a board. There was no sigh of any Chechens and early in the afternoon the order was given to retreat. The companies formed into a column behind the aoul and Butler happened to be in the rearguard. As soon as they started Chechens appeared, following and firing at the detachment, but they ceased this pursuit as soon as they came out into an open space.

Not one of Butler's company had been wounded, and he returned in a most happy and energetic mood. When after fording the same stream it had crossed in the morning, the detachment spread over the maize fields and the meadows, the singers of each company came forward and songs filled the air.

"Verry diff'rent, very diff'rent, Fagers are, Fagers are!" sang Butler's singers, and his horse stepped merrily to the music. Trezorka, the shaggy grey dog belonging to the company, ran in front, with his tail curled up with an air of responsibility like a commander. Butler felt buoyant, calm, and joyful. War presented itself to him as consisting only in his exposing himself to danger and to possible death, thereby gaining rewards and the respect of his comrades here, as well as of his friends in Russia. Strange to say, his imagination never pictured the other aspect of war: the death and wounds of the soldiers, officers, and mountaineers. To retain his poetic conception he even unconsciously avoided looking at the dead and wounded. So that day when we had three dead and twelve wounded, he passed by a corpse lying on its back and did not stop to look, seeing only with one eye the strange position of the waxen hand and a dark red spot on the head. The hosslmen appeared to him only a mounted dzhigits from whom he had to defend himself.

"You see, my dear sir," said his major in an interval between two songs, "it's not as it is with you in Petersburg — 'Eyes right! Eyes left!' Here we have done our job, and now we go home and Masha will set a pie and some nice cabbage soup before us. That's life — don't you think so? — Now then! As the Dawn Was Breaking!" He called for his favorite song.

There was no wind, the air was fresh and clear and so transparent that the snow hills nearly a hundred miles away seemed quite near, and in the intervals between the songs the regular sound of the footsteps and the jingle of the guns was heard as a background on which each song began and ended. The song that was being sung in Butler's company was composed by a cadet in honor of the regiment, and went to a dance tune. The chorus was: "Verry diff'rent, very diff'rent, Fagers are, Fagers are!"

Butler rode beside the officer next in rank above him, Major Petrov, with whom he lived, and he felt he could not be thankful enough to have exchanged from the Guards and come to the Caucasus. His chief reason for exchanging was that he had lost all he had at cards and was afraid that if he remained there he would be unable to resist playing though he had nothing more to lose. Now all that was over, his life was quite changed and was such a pleasant and brave one! He forgot that he was ruined, and forgot his unpaid debts. The Caucasus, the war, the soldiers, the officers — those tipsy, brave, good-natured fellows — and Major Petrov himself, all seemed so delightful that sometimes it appeared too good to be true that he was not in Petersburg — in a room filled with tobacco smoke, turning down the corners of cards and gambling, hating the holder of the bank and feeling a dull pain in his head — but was really here in this glorious region among these brave Caucasians.

The major and the daughter of a surgeon's orderly, formerly known as Masha, but now generally called by the more respectful name of Marya Dmitrievna, lived together as man and wife. Marya Dmitrievna was a handsome, fair-haired, very freckled, childless woman of thirty. Whatever her past may have been she was now the major's faithful companion and looked after him like a nurse — a very necessary matter, since he often drank himself into oblivion.

When they reached the fort everything happened as the major had foreseen. Marya Dmitrievna gave him and Butler, and two other officers of the detachment who had been invited, a nourishing and tasty dinner, and the major ate and drank till he was unable to speak, and then went off to his room to sleep.

Butler, having drunk rather more chikhir wine than was good for him, went to his bedroom, tired but contented, and hardly had time to undress before he fell into a sound, dreamless, and unbroken sleep with his hand under his handsome curly head.

Leo Tolstoy

Chapter XVII

The aoul which had been destroyed was that in which Hadji
Murad had spent the night before he went over to the Russians.
Sado and his family had left the aoul on the approach of the
Russian detachment, and when he returned he found his saklya
in ruins — the roof fallen in, the door and the posts supporting
the penthouse burned, and the interior filthy. His son, the
handsome bright-eyed boy who had gazed with such ecstasy at
Hadji Murad, was brought dead to the mosque on a horse
covered with a barka; he had been stabbed in the back with a
bayonet. the dignified woman who had served Hadji Murad
when he was at the house now stood over her son's body, her
smock torn in front, her withered old breasts exposed, her hair
down, and she dug her hails into her face till it bled, and wailed
incessantly. Sado, taking a pick-axe and spade, had gone with
his relatives to dig a grave for his son. The old grandfather sat
by the wall of the ruined saklya cutting a stick and gazing
stolidly in front of him. He had only just returned from the
apiary. The two stacks of hay there had been burnt, the apricot
and cherry trees he had planted and reared were broken and
scorched, and worse still all the beehives and bees had been
burnt. The wailing of the women and the little children, who

147

cried with their mothers, mingled with the lowing of the
hungry cattle for whom there was no food. The bigger children,
instead of playing, followed their elders with frightened eyes.
The fountain was polluted, evidently on purpose, so that the
water could not be used. The mosque was polluted in the same
way, and the Mullah and his assistants were cleaning it out. No
one spoke of hatred of the Russians. the feeling experienced by
all the Chechens, from the youngest to the oldest, was stronger
than hate. It was not hatred, for they did not regard those
Russian dogs as human beings, but it was such repulsion,
disgust, and perplexity at the senseless cruelty of these
creatures, that the desire to exterminate them — like the desire
to exterminate rats, poisonous spiders, or wolves — was as
natural an instinct as that of self-preservation.

The inhabitants of the aoul were confronted by the choice of
remaining there and restoring with frightful effort what had
been produced with such labor and had been so lightly and
senselessly destroyed, facing every moment the possibility of a
repetition of what had happened; or to submit to the Russians
— contrary to their religion and despite the repulsion and
contempt they felt for them. The old men prayed, and
unanimously decided to send envoys to Shamil asking him for
help. Then they immediately set to work to restore what had
been destroyed.

The second day after the raid, not too early, Butler went out
into the street by way of the back door, intending to have a
stroll and a breath of fresh air before his morning tea, which he
normally took with Petrov. The sun was already clear of the
mountains and it was painful to look at the white daub houses
where it shone on the right-hand side of the street. It was,
though, as cheering and soothing as ever to look left wards at

the black tree-clad mountains rising higher and higher in the distance and, visible beyond the ravine, the lusterless chain of snow-capped mountains pretending as always to be clouds.

Butler looked at the mountains, filled his lungs, and felt happy to be alive and to be just who he was, living in this beautiful world. He was quite happy, too, about his conduct the previous day's action, both during the advance and in particular during the march back when things were quite hot; find he was happy to recall the way Masha, otherwise Marya Dmitrievna (the woman Petrov lived with) had entertained -hem after they had got back from the raid, and the especially unaffected, kindly way she had treated everyone, being particularly nice to him, it had seemed. With her thick plait of hair, her broad shoulders, full bosom, and kindly beaming rice covered with freckles, Marya Dmitrievna could not help attracting Butler who was a, young, vigorous, unmarried man, and he even had an idea that she was keen on him. But he thought it would be a shabby way to treat his simple, good-natured comrade and always behaved towards Marya Dmitrievna with the utmost simplicity and respect and it gladdened him that he did so. He was thinking of this just now.

His thoughts were disturbed by the drumming of many horses' hoofs on the dusty road ahead of him. It sounded like several horsemen galloping. He raised his head and saw at the end of the street a party of riders approaching at a walk. There were a couple of dozen Cossacks with two men riding at their head: one wore a white cherkeska and a tall papakha wound with a turban, the other was a dark, hook-nosed officer in the Russian service, dressed in a blue cherkeska with a lavish amount of silver on his clothing and weapons. The horseman in the turban rode a handsome palomino with a small head and beautiful eyes; the officer was mounted on a tall, rather showy Karabakh. Butler, who was very keen on horses, appreciated at a glance the resilient power of the first rider's horse and stopped to find out who they were. The officer spoke to him.

'That house of commandant?' he asked, pointing with his whip at Ivan Matveevich's (Petrov's) house, and betraying by his accent and defective grammar his non-Russian origin.

'Yes, that's it,' said Butler. 'And who might that be?' he asked, going closer to the officer and with a glance indicating the man in the turban.

'That Hadji Murad. He come here and stay with commandant,' said the officer.

Butler knew about Hadji Murad and that he had surrendered to the Russians, but he had never expected to see him here, in this small fort.

Hadji Murad was looking at him in a friendly fashion.

'How do you do. KosAkoldy,' said Butler, using the Tatar greeting he had learnt.

'Saubul,' replied Hadji Murad, nodding. He rode across to Butler and offered his hand from which his whip hung on two fingers.

'Commandant?' he asked.

'No, the commandant is inside. I'll go and fetch him,' Butler said to the officer, going up the steps and pushing at the door.

But the 'front door', as Marya Dmitrievna called it, was locked. Butler knocked, but getting no reply went round by the back way. He called for his batman, but got no answer, and being unable to find either of the two boatman went into the kitchen. Marya Dmitrievna was there, with face flushed, her hair pinned up in a kerchief and sleeves rolled up over her plump, white arms. she was cutting pie-cases from a rolled out layer of dough as white as her arms.

'Where have the batmen got to?' asked Butler.

'Gone off drinking,' said Marya Dmitrievna. 'What is it you want?'

'I want the door opened. You've got a whole horde of mountaineers outside. Hadji Murad has come.'

'Go on, tell me another one,' said Marya Dmitrievna, smiling.

'It's not a joke. It's true. They are just outside.'

'What? Really?' said Marya Dmitricvna.

'Why should I want to make it up? Go and look — they are just outside.

'Well, there's a thing!' said Marya Dmitrievna, rolling down her sleeves and feeling for the pins in her thick plait of hair. 'I'll go and wake up Ivan Matvcovich, then!'

'No, I'll go. You, Bondarenko, go and open the door,' said Butler.

'That's all right by me,' said Marya Dmitrievna and returned to her work.

When he learnt that Hadji Murad had arrived, Petrov, who had heard already that he was in Grozny, was not in the least surprised. He sat up in bed, rolled a cigarette, lit it, and began to get dressed, loudly coughing to clear his throat and grumbling at the higher-ups who had sent 'that devil' to him. When he was dressed, he ordered his batman to bring his ' medicine ', and the batman, knowing what he meant, brought him some vodka.

'You should never mix your drinks,' he growled, drinking the vodka and eating a piece of black bread with it. 'I was drinking chikhir last night and now I've got a thick head. All right, I'm ready,' he said finally and went into the parlor, where Butler had taken Hadji Murad and the escorting officer.

The officer handed Ivan Matveevich the orders from the commander of the Left Flank in which he was instructed to take charge of Hadji Murad and, while allowing him contact with the mountaineers through scouts, to ensure that he never left the fort except with an escort of Cossacks.

Ivan Matveevich read the paper, looked hard at Hadji Murad, and studied the paper again. After several times shifting his gaze from the paper to his visitor, he finally fixed his eyes on Hadji Murad and said:

'Yakshi, bek-yaksh~. Very well. Let him stay then. But you tell him that my orders are not to let him loose. And orders are orders. As to quarters, what do you think, Butler? We could put him in the office.'.'

Before Butler could reply, Marya Dmitrievna, who had come from the kitchen and was standing in the doorway, said to Ivan Matveevich:

'Why in the office? Let him stay here. We can give him the guest-room and the store-room. At least he'll be where you can keep an eye on him,' she said. she glanced at Hadji Murad, but meeting his eyes turned hurriedly away.

'Yes, I think Marya Dmitrievna is right,' said Butler.

'Go on, off with you!' said Ivan Matveevich, frowning 'Womenfolk have no business here.'

Throughout this conversation Hadji Murad sat with his hand behind the handle of his dagger and a faintly disdainful smile on his lips. He said it mattered nothing where he lived. All he needed was what the sardar had granted — to have contact with the mountaineers, and he wished therefore that they be allowed access to him. Ivan Matveevich said that this would be done and asked Butler to look after their guests while something to eat was brought and the rooms made ready. He would go to the office to fill in the necessary papers and give the necessary instructions.

Hadji Murat's relations with these new acquaintances immediately became very clearly established. From their first meeting Hadji Murat felt nothing but repugnance and scorn for Ivan Matveevich and was always haughty in his treatment of him. He particularly liked Marya Dn1itrievna, who cooked and

153

served his food. He liked her simple manner, her particular, for him foreign, type of beauty, and the unconsciously conveyed attraction which she felt for him. He tried not to look at her, or to speak to her, but his eyes turned automatically towards her and followed her movements.

With Butler he struck up an immediate friendship and took pleasure in the long talks he had with him, asking Butler about his life and telling him of his own, passing on the news brought by the scouts about the situation of his family and even asking his advice as to what he should do.

The news brought by the scouts was not good. In the four days he had been at the fort they had come twice and on both occasions the news was bad.

Shortly after Hadji Murad's surrender to the Russians his family was taken to the village of Vedeno and kept there under guard waiting for Shamil to decide their fate. The women — Hadji Murad's old mother Patimat and his two wives — together with their five small children lived under guard in the house of Ibrahim Rashid, one of Shamil's captains; Yusuf, his eighteen-year-old son, was kept in a dungeon, a deep pit dug eight or nine feet into the ground, with four criminals who, like him, were awaiting Shamil's decision on their fate.

But no decision came, because Shamil was away campaigning against the Russians.

On 6 January 1852, Shamil returned home to Vedeno after a battle with the Russians in which, according to the Russians, he had been beaten and fled to Vedeno, but in which, according to the view of Shamil and all his murids, he had been victorious and put the Russians to flight. In this engagement and it happened very rarely — he himself had fired his rifle and with drawn sword would have charged straight at the Russians if his escort of murids had not held him back. Two of them were killed at his side.

It was midday when Shamil arrived at his destination, surrounded by his party of murids showing of their horsemanship, firing rifles and pistols and chanting endlessly 'La ilaha illa allah.'

All the people of Vedeno, which was a large village, were standing in the street and on the roofs of the houses to greet their master, and they too celebrated the event with musket and pistol fire. Shamil rode on a white Arab, which merrily sought to have its head as they neared home. The horse's harness was extremely plain with no gold or silver ornament a red leather bridle, finely made and grooved down the middle, metal bucket stirrups and a red shabrack showing from under the saddle. The Imam wore a fur coat overlaid with brown cloth, the black fur projecting at the collar and cuffs; it was drawn tight about his tall, slim frame by a black leather strap with a dagger attached to it. On his head he wore a tall, flattopped papakha with a black tassel and white turban round it, the end of which hung below his neck. On his feet were green soft leather boots and his legs were covered with tight black leggings edged with plain lace.

The Iman wore nothing at all that glittered, no gold or silver, and his tall, erect, powerful figure in its plain clothes in the midst of the murids with their gold- and silver-ornamented dress and weapons, created on the people exactly the impression of grandeur which he desired and knew how to create His pale face, framed by his trimmed red beard, with its small, constantly screwed up eyes, wore a fixed expression as if made of stone. Passing through the village he felt thousands of eyes turned on him, but his own eyes looked at no one. The wives and children of Hadji Murad went on to the verandah with the other occupants of the house to watch the Imam's entry. Only Patimat, Hadji Murad's old mother, did not go, but remained sitting as she was on the floor of the house with her grey hair disheveled and her long arms clasped round her thin knees, while she blinked her fiery black eyes and watched the logs burning down in the fire-place. She, like her son, had always hated Shamil, now more than ever, and had no wish to see him.

Hadji Murad's son also saw nothing of Shamil's triumphal entry. From his dark fetid pit he could only hear the shots and chanting and he experienced such anguish as is only felt by young men, full of life, when deprived of their freedom. Sitting in the stinking pit and seeing only the same wretched, filthy, emaciated creatures he was confined with, who mostly hated one another, he was overcome by a passionate envy for people who had air and light and freedom and were at this moment prancing round their leader on dashing horses and shooting and chanting in chorus 'La ilaha illa allah.'

After processing through the village Shamil rode into a large courtyard next to an inner one where he had his harem. Two armed Lezghians met Shamil at the opened gates of the first courtyard. The yard was full of people. There were people from distant parts here on their own account, there were petitioners, and there were those whom Shamil himself had summoned for judgement. When Shamil rode in everyone in the courtyard rose and respectfully greeted the Imam with their hands placed to their chests. Some knelt and remained kneeling while Shamil crossed the courtyard from the outer to the inner gateway. Although Shamil recognized in the waiting crowd many disagreeable people and many tiresome petitioners who would be wanting his attention, he rode past them with the same stony expression on his face and went into the inner court where he dismounted alongside the veranda of his residence to the left of the gate.

The campaign had been a strain, mental rather than physical, for although he had proclaimed it a victory, Shamil knew that the campaign had been a failure, that many Chechen villages had been burnt and destroyed, and that the Chechens — a fickle and light-headed people — were wavering and some of them, nearest to the Russians, were already prepared to go over to them. It was all very difficult and measures would have to be taken, but for the moment Shamil did not want to do anything or think about anything. All he wanted was to relax and enjoy the soothing delights of family life provided by his favorite wife Aminet, a black-eyed, fleet-footed Kist girl of eighteen.

But not only was it out of the question to see Aminet at this moment — though she was only on the other side of the fence which separated the women's apartments from the men's quarters in the inner courtyard (and Shamil had no doubt that even as he dismounted Aminet and his other wives would be watching through the fence) — not only could he not go to her, he could not even lie down on a feather mattress and recover from his fatigue. Before anything else he had to perform his midday devotions. He felt not the least inclination to do so, but it was necessary that he should, not only in his capacity as religious leader of the people, but also because to him personally it was as essential as his daily food. So he carried out the ritual washing and praying. At the end of the prayers he summoned those who were waiting.

The first to come in to him was his father-in-law and teacher, Jemel-Edin, a tall fine-looking old man with grey hair, snowy white beard and a rubicund face. After a prayer to God, he began to question Shamil about the campaign and to recount what had happened in the mountains while he was away.

There were all manner of events to report — blood-feud killings, cattle-stealing, alleged breaches of the Tarikat — smoking tobacco, drinking wine, and Jemel-Edin also told Shamil that Hadji Murad had sent men to take his family over to the Russians, but that this was discovered and the family had been moved to Vedeno, where they were now under guard awaiting the Imam's decision. The old men were gathered in the adjoining guest-room for the purpose of considering all these matters, and Jemel-Edin advised Shamil to dismiss them today since they had already waited three days for him.

Shamil took dinner in his own room, where it was brought by Zaidet, the senior of his wives, a sharp-nosed, dark, ill-favored woman for whom he did not care. He then went into the guest-room.

There were six men in Shamil's council — old men with white, grey and ginger beards. They wore tall papakhas with or without turbans, new jackets and cherkeskass with leather belts and daggers. They rose to greet him. Shamil was a head taller than any of them. They all, including Shamil, lifted their upturned hands and with closed eyes recited a prayer, then wiped their hands across their faces, drew them down over their beards and joined them. This done, they sat down, with

Shamil sitting on a higher cushion in the middle, and began their deliberations of the business in hand.

The cases of those accused of crimes were decided according to the Shariat: two thieves were condemned to have a hand cut off, another to have his head cut off for murder, and three were pardoned. They moved on then to the main business to consider what measures should be taken to prevent the Chechens going over to the Russians. In order to halt these defections Jemel-Edin had drawn up the following proclamation:

'May you have peace everlasting with Almighty God. I hear that the Russians show favors to you and call for your submission. Believe them not, do not submit, but be patient. For this you will be rewarded, if not in this life, then in the life to come. Remember what happened before when your weapons were taken from you. If then, in 1840, God had not shown you the light, you would now be soldiers and carry bayonets instead of daggers, and your wives would not wear trousers and would be defiled. Judge the future by the past. It is better to die at war with the Russians than to live with the infidels. Be patient, and I shall come with the Koran and the sword to lead you against the Russians. For the present I strictly command you to have neither intention nor even any thought of submitting to the Russians.'

Shamil approved the proclamation, signed it and decreed that it should be dispatched to all parts.

When this business was finished the question of Hadji Murad was discussed. This was a very important matter for Shamil. Although he did not care to admit it, he knew that if Hadji

Murad had been on his side, with his skill, daring, and courage what had now happened in Chechnia would never have occurred. It would be good to settle his quarrel with Hadji Murad and make use of him once again; but if that could not be done, he must still ensure that he did not aid the Russians. In either case, therefore, he must send for him and, when he came, kill him. This could be done either by sending a man to Tiflis to kill him there, or by summoning him and putting an end to him here. The only way to do that was to use Hadji Murad's family, above all his son, whom, as Shamil knew, he adored. It was therefore necessary to work through his son.

When the councilors had talked it over, Shamil closed his eyes and fell silent.

The councilors knew what this meant: Shamil was now listening to the voice of the Prophet telling him what should be done. After five minutes' solemn silence Shamil opened his eyes, screwing them more tightly than before and said:

'Fetch me the son of Hadji Murad.'

'He is here,' said Jemel-Edin.

Indeed, Yusuf, thin, pale, ragged, and stinking, still handsome though in face and figure, and with the same fiery black eyes as Patimat, his grandmother, was standing at the gate of the outer courtyard waiting to be summoned.

Yusuf did not feel about Shamil as his father did. He did not know all that had happened in the past, or if he knew, it was only at second-hand, and he could not understand why his father was so doggedly opposed to Shamil. Yusuf only wanted to go on living the easy, rakish life that he, as son of the naib, had led in Khunzakh, and he could see no point in being at odds with Shamil. In defiant opposition to his father he greatly admired Shamil and regarded him with the fervent veneration that was generally felt for him in the mountains. He experienced a particular feeling of awe and reverence for the Imam now as he entered the guest-room. He stopped at the door and was fixed by Shamil's screwed up eyes. He stood for a few moments, then went up to Shamil and kissed his large white hand with long fingers.

'You are the son of Hadji Murad?'

'Yes, Imam.'

'You know what he has done?'

'I know, Imam, and am sorry for it.'

'Do you know how to write?'

'I was studying to be a mullah.'

'Then write to your father and say that if he returns to me now, before Bairam, I will pardon him and all will be as of old. But if he will not and remains with the Russians, then . . ,' — Shamil frowned menacingly — 'I shall give your grandmother and mother to be used in the villages, and I shall cut off your head.'

Not a muscle twitched on Yusuf's face. He bowed his head to signify he had understood what Shamil said.

'Write that and give it to my messenger.'

Shamil was then silent and took a long look at Yusuf

'Write that I have decided to spare you. I will not kill you but will have your eyes put out, the same as I do to all traitors. Go.'

Yusuf appeared to be calm while in the presence of Shamil, but when he was led out of the guest-room he threw himself on his escort, snatched his dagger from its sheath and tried to kill himself But he was seized by the arms, bound and taken back to the pit.

That evening when the evening prayers were over and dusk fell, Shamil put on a white fur top-coat and passed through the fence into the part of the courtyard where his wives lived. He went straight to Aminet's room. But Aminet was not there; she was with the older wives. Trying to keep out of sight, Shamil stood behind the door of her room to wait for her. But Aminet was angry with Shamil because he had given some silk to Zaidet and not to her. she saw him come out and go to look for her in her room and she deliberately did not return to her room. she stood a long time in Zaidet's doorway, laughing quietly as she watched the white figure go in and out of her room. It was nearly time for the midnight prayers when Shamil, after waiting in vain, went back to his own quarters.

Hadji Murad had been a week at the fort living in the house of Ivan Matveevich. Although Marya Dmitrievna had quarreled with the shaggy-haired Khanefi (Hadji Murad had with him only two men: Khanefi and Eldar) and had several times ejected him from her kitchen — for which he nearly cut her throat — she evidently felt a particular respect and sympathetic concern for Hadji Murad. She no longer served him his dinner, a task she had passed on to Eldar, but she took every opportunity to see him and do anything she could to please him. she also took a very keen interest in the negotiations about his family; she knew how many wives he had, how many children and what ages they were, and each time a scout came she asked whom she could to discover how the negotiations were going.

In the course of this week Butler had become firm friends with Hadji Murad. Sometimes Hadji Murad would call on him in his room, at other times Butler would visit him. They sometimes conversed through an interpreter, otherwise they used their own resources — signs and, particularly, smiles. Hadji Murad had evidently taken a liking to Butler. This was clear from the way that Butler was treated by Eldar. Whenever Butler came into Hadji Murad's room Eldar greeted him, flashing his teeth in a cheerful grin, hastened to put cushions on his seat and helped him off with his sword if he was wearing

Butler also got on good terms with the shaggy-haired Khanefi, who was Hadji Murad's sworn brother. Khanefi knew many songs of the mountains and sang them well. To please Butler Hadji Murad would summon Khanefi and tell him to sing, mentioning the songs he thought good. Khanefi had a high tenor voice and sang with great clarity and expression. There was one song Hadji Murad was particularly fond of and Butler was much struck by its solemn, sad refrain. Butler asked the interpreter to tell him the words in Russian and wrote it down.

The song was about vengeance — the vengeance that Khanefi and Hadji Murad had pledged to each other.

It went as follows:

'The earth will dry on my grave, and you, my own mother, will forget me. Grave grass will grow over the graveyard and will deaden your grief, my old father. The tears will dry in my sister's eyes and sorrow will fly from her heart.

'But you, my elder brother, will not forget me till you have avenged my death. You, my second brother, will not forget me till you lie by my side.

'Bullet, you are hot and the bearer of death, but were you not my faithful slave? Black earth, you will cover me, but did I not trample you beneath my horse's hoofs? Death, you are cold, but I was your master. The earth shall take my body, and heaven my soul.'

Hadji Murad always listened to this song with his eyes closed, and, as its last lingering note faded away, he would say in Russian:

'Good song, wise song.'

With the arrival of Hadji Murad and his close acquaintance with him and his murids, Butler was even more captivated by the poetry of the peculiar, vigorous life led by the mountaineers. He got himself a jacket, cherkeska and leggings, and he felt he was a mountaineer too, living the same life as these people.

On the day Hadji Murad was to leave Ivan Matveevich gathered a few of the officers to see him off. The officers were sitting at two tables, one for tea, dispensed by Marya

Hadji Murad

Dmitrievna, and the other laid with vodka, chikhir and hors d'oeuvre, when Hadji Murad, armed and dressed for the road, came limping with quick, soft steps into the room.

Everyone rose and one after the other shook hands with him. Ivan Matveevich invited hem to sit on the ottoman, but Hadji Murad thanked him and sat on a chair by the window He was clearly not in the least put out by the silence which fell when he came in. He closely studied the faces of those present then fixed his eyes indifferently on the table with the samovar and food on it. Petrokovsky, one of the officers more spirited than the rest, who had not seen Hadji Murad before, asked him through the interpreter if he had liked Tiflis.

Maya,' said Hadji Murad.

'He says he does,' the interpreter answered.

'What did he like in particular?'

Hadji Murad made some reply.

'He liked the theater best.'

'Did he enjoy the commander-in-chief's ball?'

Hadji Murad frowned.

'Every people has its own customs. Our women do not wear such clothes,' he said, glancing at Marya Dmitrievna.

'What didn't he like?'

'We have a saying,' Hadji Murad said to the interpreter. 'A dog asked a donkey to eat with him and gave him meat, the donkey asked the dog and gave him hay: they both went hungry.' He smiled. ' Every people finds its own ways good.'

The conversation stopped there. The officers began drinking tea or eating. Hadji Murad took the glass of tea he was offered and put it in front of him.

'Now, would you like some cream? Perhaps a bun?' asked Marya Dmitrievna, serving him.

Hadji Murad inclined his head.

'Well, good-bye then,' said Butler, touching him on the knee. 'When shall we meet again?'

'Good-bye, good-bye,' Hadji Murad said in Russian, smiling. 'Kunak Bulur. I your good kunak. Now time — off we go,' he said, tossing his head as if to show the direction he had to go. Eldar appeared in the doorway with something large and white over his shoulder and a sword in his hand. Hadji Murad beckoned him and Eldar with his long strides came over and gave him the white cloak and the sword. Hadji Murad took the cloak and, dropping it over his arm, gave it to Marya Dmitrievnas saying something for the interpreter to translates

'He says: you admired the cloak — take it,' said the interpreter.

'But what for?' said Marya Dmitrievna, blushing.

'Must do. Adat tad it is the custom', said Hadji Murad.

'Well, thank you,' said Marya Dmitrievna, taking the cloak. '
God grant you may rescue your son. He is a fine boy ulan
yakshi,' she added. 'Tell him I hope he can rescue his family.'

Hadji Murad looked at Marya Dmitrievna and nodded in
approval. Then he took the sword from Eldar and gave it to
Ivan Matveevich. Ivan Matveevich took it and said to the
interpreter:

'Tell him he must take my brown gelding. That is all I can give
in return.'

Hadji Murad waved his hand in front of his face to show that
he did not want anything and would not accept it. Then he
pointed first to the mountains, then to his heart, and went to the
door. Everyone followed. Some of the officers, who remained
inside, drew the sword and after inspecting the blade decided it
was a genuine gourda.

Butler accompanied Hadji Murad on to the steps outside. But
just then something totally unexpected happened which might
have cost Hadji Murad his life but for his promptness,
determination and skill.

The villagers of Tash-Kichu, a Kumyk village, held Hadji
Murad in high esteem and on many occasions had come to the
fort just to have a look at the celebrated naib. Three days
before Hadji Murad's departure they sent messengers inviting
him to attend their mosque on Friday. However, the Kumyk
princes who resided at Tash-Kichu hated Hadji Murad and had
a blood feud with him, and when they heard of the villagers'
invitation they would not allow him into the mosque. The
people were roused by this and there was a fight between the

villagers and the princes' supporters. The Russian authorities restored peace among the mountaineers and sent a message to Hadji Murad instructing him not to attend the mosque. Hadji Murad did not go and everybody thought the matter was ended.

But at the very moment of Hadji Murad's departure, when he went out on to the steps and the horses stood waiting outside, one of the Kumyk princes, Arslan-Khan, who was known to Butler and Ivan Matveevich, rode up to the house.

Seeing Hadji Murad he drew his pistol from his belt and aimed it at him. But before Arslan-Khan could fire, Hadji Murad, despite his lameness, sprang like a cat from the steps towards him. Arslan-Khan fired and missed. Hadji Murad meanwhile had run up to him, and with one hand seized his horse's bridle and with the other pulled out his dagger, shouting something in Tatar.

Butler and Eldar rushed up to the enemies at the same time and seized them by the arms. Hearing the shot, Ivan Matveevich also appeared.

'What do you mean by this, Arslan — creating mischief in my house!' he said, on discovering what had happened. ' It's no way to behave. Have it out with each other by all means, but keep it "out" and don't go slaughtering people in my house.'

Arslan-Khan, a tiny man with a black mustache, got down from his horse, pale and shaking, and with a vicious look at Hadji Murad went off with Ivan Matveevich into the parlor. Hadji Murad went back to the horses, breathing heavily and smiling.

'Why did he want to kill you?' Butler asked him through the interpreter. The interpreter translated Hadji Murad's reply: 'He says that it is our law. Arslan has blood to avenge on him, that is why he wanted to kill him.'

'And what if he catches up with him on his journey?' asked Butler.

Hadji Murad smiled.

'What of it? If he kills me, it will be the will of Allah. Well, good-bye,' he said once more in Russian, and grasping his horse by the withers, looked round at those seeing him off and affectionately encountered Marya Dnzitrievna's eye.

'Good-bye, good lady,' he said to her. ' Thank you.'

'May God only grant you can get your family free,' repeated Marya Dmitrievna.

Hadji Murad did not understand what she said, but he understood her concern for him and nodded to her.

'Be sure you don't forget your ktlnak,' said Butler.

'Tell him I am his true friend and will never forget him,' Hadji Murad replied through the interpreter. Then, despite his crooked leg, as soon as his foot touched the stirrup he swung his body quickly and effortlessly on to the high saddle and, straightening his sword and with a customary hand fingering his pistol, he rode off from Ivan Matveevich's house with that particular proud, warlike air the mountaineers have when on horseback. Khanefi and Eldar also mounted and, after bidding friendly farewells to their hosts and the officers, set off at a trot after their murshid.

As always happens, a discussion started about the person who had left.

'He's a great fellow!'

'It was just like a wolf the way he went for Arslan-Khan. There was a completely different look on his face.'

'He will do us down,' said Petrokovsky. ' He must be a right rogue.'

'Then I wish there were more Russian rogues like him,' interposed Marya Dmitrievna with sudden annoyance. 'He was with us for a week and he couldn't have been nicer,' she said. 'Polite and wise and fair-minded he was.'

'How did you find all that out?'

'I just did.'

'Fallen for him, have you?' said Ivan Matveevich, coming in. 'It's a fact.'

'All right, so I've fallen for him. What's that to you? I just don't see why you speak ill of somebody when he is a good man. He may be a Tatar, but he is a good man.'

'Quite right, Marya Dmitrievna,' said Butler. 'Good for you to stand up for him.

The life of those living in the advanced fortresses on the Chechnia Line went on as before. In the interval there had been two alarms; foot-soldiers came running out, Cossacks and militia galloped in pursuit, but on neither occasion were they able to apprehend the mountaineers. They got away, and on one occasion at Vozdvizhenskoe drove off eight Cossack horses which were being watered and killed a Cossack. There had been no Russian raids since the one which had destroyed the village. But a major expedition into Greater Chechnia was expected following the appointment of Prince Baryatinsky as commander of the Left Flank.

On arriving in Grozny, being now in command of the whole Left Flank, Prince Baryatinsky (a friend of the Crown Prince and former commander of the Kabarda Regiment) at once assembled a force to continue the fulfillment of the Emperor's instructions which Chernyshev had communicated to Vorontsov. The column set out from Vozdvizhenskoe, where it had assembled, and took up position on the road to Kurinskoe. The troops camped there and engaged in forest clearing.

Young Vorontsov lived in a magnificent fabric tent; his wife, Marya Vasilevna, would drive out to the camp and often stayed overnight. Baryatinsky's relations with Marya Vasilevna were a matter of common knowledge, and she was coarsely abused by the officers unconnected with the court and by the ordinary soldiers, who because of her presence in the camp were sent out on night picket duty. It was usual for the mountaineers to bring up their cannon and fire into the camp. The shots they fired mostly missed their target so as a rule no action was taken against them. But to prevent the mountaineers bringing up their guns and frightening Marya Vasilevna pickets were sent out. To go on picket every night to save a lady from being frightened was an insult and an offense, and the soldiers and the officers not received in the best society had some choice names for Marya Vasilevna.

Butler took leave from the fort and paid a visit to the column in order to see old comrades from the Corps of Pages and his regiment, now serving in the Kura Regiment or as aides-de-camp or adjutants on the stay He found it all very enjoyable from the start. He stayed in Poltoratsky's tent and there found a number of people he knew who were delighted to see him. He also went to see Vorontsov, whom he knew slightly, having once served in the same regiment with him. Vorontsov made him very welcome. He introduced him to Prince Baryatinsky and invited him to the farewell dinner he was giving to General Kozlovsky, Baryatinsky's predecessor as commander of the Left Flank.

The dinner was splendid. Six tents had been brought up and pitched together in a row. Their whole length was taken up by a table laid with cutlery, glasses and bottles. It was all reminiscent of the guards officers' life in St Petersburg. They sat down to table at two o'clock. In the center of the table sat Kozlovsky on one side, and Baryatinsky on the other. Vorontsov sat on Kozlovsky's right, his wife on his left. The whole length of the table on either side was filled by officers of the Kabarda and Kura Regiments. Butler sat by Poltoratsky and they chatted gaily and drank with the officers sitting by them. When they got to the main course and the orderlies began filling the glasses with champagne, Poltoratsky — with genuine apprehension and regret — said to Butler.

'Old "um-er" is going to make a fool of himself'

'What do you mean?'

'Why, he's got to make a speech. And how can he?'

'Yes, old boy, it's a bit different from capturing barricades under fire. And on top of that he's got the lady next to him and all these court fellows. It really is pitiful to watch,' said the officers one to another.

But the solemn moment arrived. Baryatinsky rose and, lifting his glass, addressed a short speech to Kozlovsky. When he had finished, Kozlovsky got up and in a reasonably firm voice began to speak:

'By his Imperial Majesty's command I am leaving you, gentlemen,' he said. ' we are parting, but always consider me um-er — present with you . . . You, gentlemen, know the truth of the — um-er — saying that you cannot soldier on your own. And so all the rewards that have come to me in my — um-er service, everything that has been — um-er — bestowed upon me, the generous tokens of his Majesty's favor, my — um-er position, and my — um-er — good name, all this, absolutely everything' — his voice quivered — 'I — um-er — owe to you and to you alone, my dear friends.' And his wrinkled face wrinkled still more, he gave a sob, and tears came to his eyes. 'I give you my — um-er — sincere and heartfelt thanks . . .'

Kozlovsky could not go on and stood to embrace the officers who came up to him. Everyone was very touched. The princess covered her face with her handkerchief Prince Vorontsov pulled a face and blinked hard. Many of the officers, too, were moved to tears. And Butler, who did not know Kozlovsky well, was also unable to restrain himself. He found it all exceptionally agreeable. After this there were toasts to Baryatinsky, to Vorontsov, to the officers, to the other ranks, and finally the guests left, intoxicated by wine and the rapturous martial sentiment to which they were anyway specially inclined.

The weather was superb — sunny and calm, and the air fresh and invigorating. On every side was the sound of campfires crackling and men singing. Everyone seemed to be celebrating. Butler went to call on Poltoratsky in the most happy and serene frame of mind. Some of the officers were gathered there, a card-table had been set up and an aide-decamp had gone banker with a hundred rubles. Twice Butler left the tent holding on to the purse in the pocket of his trousers, but in the end he succumbed and, despite the vow he had made to his brothers and to himself, began playing against the bank.

Before an hour was past Butler, flushed and sweating, covered with chalk, was sitting with his elbows on the table, writing down his bets beneath the crumpled cards. He had lost so much that he was now afraid of counting what was scored against him. He knew without reckoning that if he used all the pay he could get in advance and whatever his horse would fetch he could still not make up the whole of what he owed to this unknown aide-de-camp. He would have gone on playing, but the aide-de-camp put down the cards with his clean white hands and began totting up the column of chalk entries under Butler's name. Butler with embarrassment apologized that he was unable to pay all his losses immediately and said he would send the money on; as he said it he saw they were all sorry for him and everyone, even Poltoratsky, avoided his gaze. It was his last evening. All he had to do was to avoid gambling and go to Vorontsov's where he had been invited. Everything would have been fine, he thought. But far from being fine, everything now was disastrous.

After saying good-bye to his comrades and friends, he left for home and on arriving went straight to bed and slept for eighteen hours at a stretch, as people usually do after losing heavily. Marya Dmitrievna could tell he had lost everything by his request for fifty kopecks to tip his Cossack escort, by his melancholy look and terse replies, and she set on Ivan Matveevich for giving him leave.

It was after eleven when Butler woke on the following day and when he recalled the situation he was in he would have liked to sink back into the oblivion from which he had just emerged, but this could not be done. He had to take steps to repay the 470 rubles which he owed to this total stranger. One step was to write a letter to his brother, repenting for his misdeed and begging him to send for the last time 500 rubles on account of his share in the mill which they still owned jointly. Then he wrote to a skinflint relative begging her to let him have 500 rubles, too, at whatever interest she wanted. Then he went to see Ivan Matveevich and knowing that he, or rather Marya Dmitrievna, had money, asked for a loan of 500 rubles.

'I'd be glad to: I'd let you have it like a shot, but Masha wouldn't part with it. These damned womenfolk are that tight-fisted. But you've got to get off the hook somehow. What about that sutler, hasn't he got any money?'

But there was no point even trying to borrow from the sutler, so Butler's only source of salvation was his brother or the skinflint relative. Having failed to achieve his purpose in Chechnia, Hadji Murad returned to Tiflis. He went daily to see

Vorontsov, and when Vorontsov received him he begged him to collect the mountaineers held captive and exchange them for his family. He repeated again that unless this were done he was tied and could not, as he wished, serve the Russians and destroy Shamil. Vorontsov promised in general terms to do what he could, but deferred giving a decision until General Argutinsky arrived in Tiflis and he could discuss it with him. Hadji Murad then asked Vorontsov's permission to go for a time to Nukha, a small town in Transcaucasia where he thought it would be easier to conduct negotiations about his family with Shamil and his supporters. Besides that, Nukha was a Muslim town with a mosque and it would be easier for him there to perform the prayers required by Muslim law. Vorontsov wrote to St Petersburg about this, and meanwhile allowed Hadji Murad to go to Nukha.

The story of Hadji Murad was regarded by Vorontsov, by the authorities in St Petersburg and by the majority of Russians who knew of it either as a lucky turn in the course of the war in the Caucasus or simply as an interesting episode. But for Hadji Murad, especially more recently, it was a drastic turning-point in his life. He had fled from the mountains partly to save his life and partly because of his hatred for Shamil. Despite all difficulties, he had succeeded in escaping, and initially he had been delighted with his success and actually considered his plans for attacking Shamil. But getting his family out, which he had supposed would be easy, had proved harder than he thought. Shamil had seized his family and now held them captive, promising to dispatch the women into the villages and to kill or blind his son. Now Hadji Murad was going to Nukha to try with the help of his supporters in Daghestan by guile or force to rescue his family from Shamil. The last scout to call on him at Nukha told him that the Avars who were loyal to him were going to carry off his family and bring them over to the Russians, but as they were short of men ready to undertake this they were reluctant to attempt it in Vedeno where the family was held and would only do it if they were moved from Vedeno to some other place. They would then take action while they were being moved. Hadji Murad ordered him to tell his friends that he would give 3,000 rubles for the release of his family.

At Nukha Hadji Murad was allotted a small house with five rooms not far from the mosque and the khan's palace. Living in the same house were the officers and interpreter attached to him and his nukers. Hadji Murad spent his time waiting for and receiving the scouts who came in from the mountains and in going for the rides he was allowed to take in the neighbor hood of Nukha.

On 8 April when he returned from riding Hadji Murad learnt that in his absence an official had arrived from Tiflis. Despite his anxiety to find out what news the official brought him, Hadji Murad did not go at once to the room where the official and the local commissioner were waiting, but went first to his own room to say his midday prayers. After he had prayed, he went into the other room which served him as a sitting-room and reception room. The official from Tiflis, a chubby state councilor called Kirillov, conveyed to him that Vorontsov wished him to be in Tiflis by the twelfth for a meeting with Argutinsky.

'Yakshi,' said Hadji Murad sharply.

He did not take to this official Kirillov.

'Have you brought the money?'

'Yes, I have it,' said Kirillov.

'It is for two weeks now,' said Hadji Murad, holding up ten fingers then four more. ' Give it to me.'

'You will have it directly,' said the official, getting a purse from his traveling bag. 'What does he want money for?' he said to the commissioner in Russian, presuming that Hadji Murad would not understand. But Hadji Murad did understand and looked angrily at Kirillov. As he was taking out the money Kirillov, who wanted to strike up some conversation with Hadji Murad in order to have something to report to Vorontsov on his return, asked him through the interpreter if he found life tedious in Nukha. Hadji Murad gave a scornful sideways glance at this fat little man in civilian clothes who carried no weapons, and made no answer. The interpreter repeated the question.

'Tell him I have nothing to say to him. Let him just give me the money.'

With this, Hadji Murad again sat down at the table and prepared to count the money.

When Kirillov had produced the gold ten-ruble pieces and laid out seven piles each of ten coins (Hadji Murad received 50 rubles in gold per day), he pushed them across to Hadji Murad. Hadji Murad dropped the coins into the sleeve of his eherkeska, rose and, as he left the room, quite unexpectedly rapped the state councilor on the top of his bald head. The state councilor leapt to his feet and commanded the interpreter to say that he had better not treat him like that because he was equivalent in rank to a colonel. The commissioner agreed. Hadji Murad merely nodded to indicate that he knew that and left the room.

'What can you do with him?' said the commissioner. 'He will stick his dagger in you, and that's that. There's no coming to terms with these devils. And he's getting his blood up, I can see.'

As soon as dusk fell two scouts, hooded to the eyes, came in from the mountains. The commissioner took them into Hadji Murad's quarters. One of the scouts was a dark, portly Tavlistani, the other a skinny old man. For Hadji Murad the news they brought was cheerless. Those of his friends who had undertaken to rescue his family were now backing out completely for fear of Shamil, who threatened the most horrifying deaths to any who helped Hadji Murad. Having heard their account, Hadji Murad put his elbows on his crossed legs, bowed his head (he was wearing his papakha) and for a long time was silent. He was thinking, thinking positively. He knew that he was thinking now for the last time, that he must reach a decision. Hadji Murad raised his head and, taking two gold pieces, gave one to each of the scouts.

'Go now.'

'What will be the answer?'

'The answer will be as God wills. Go.'

The scouts got up and left. Hadji Murad remained sitting on the rug, his elbows on his knees. He sat there for a long time.

'What should I do? Trust Shamil and go back to him? He is a fox and would play me false. And even if he did not, I could still not submit to this ginger-haired double-dealer. I could not because, now that I have been with the Russians, he will never trust me again,' thought Hadji Murad.

And he recalled the Tavlistan folk-tale about the falcon which was caught, lived among people and then returned to his home in the mountains. The falcon returned wearing jesses on his legs and there were bells still on them. And the falcons spurned him. 'Fly back to the place where they put silver bells on you,' they said. ' we have no bells, nor do we have jesses.' The falcon did not want to leave his homeland and stayed. But the other falcons would not have him and tore him to death.

Just as they will tear me to death, thought Hadji Murad.

'Should I stay here? Win the Caucasus for the Russian tsar, gain fame and wealth and titles?'

'Yes, I could do that,' he thought, recalling his meetings with Vorontsov and the old prince's flattering words.

'But I have to decide now, or he will destroy my family.'

All night Hadji Murad was awake, thinking.

Half-way through the night he had made up his mind. He decided that he must flee to the mountains and with the Avars who were loyal to him force his way into Vedeno and either free his family or die in the attempt. Whether or not to bring his family back to the Russians or flee to Khunzakh with them and

fight Shamil he did not decide. He knew only that he must now
get away from the Russians and into the mountains. And he
began at once to put this decision into effect. He took his black
quilted jacket from beneath the cushion and went to his nukers'
quarters. They lived across the hall. As soon as he stepped out
into the hall, the door of which was open, he was enveloped by
the dewy freshness of the moonlit night and his ears were filled
by the whistling and warbling of nightingales in the garden by
the house.

Hadji Murad crossed the hall and opened the door of his
nukers' room. There was no light in the room, only the new
moon in its first quarter shining through the windows. A table
and two chairs stood to the side and all four nukers lay on rugs
and cloaks spread on the floor. Khanefi was sleeping outside
with the horses. Gamzalo, hearing the door creak, raised
himself, looked around and, seeing it was Hadji Murad, lay
down again. Eldar, however, who lay next to him sprang up
and began to put on his jacket, expecting some command.
Kurban and Khan-Mahoma slept on. Hadji Murad put hisj
jacket on the table and there was the knock of something hard
as he did so: the gold pieces sewn in the lining.

'Sew these in as well,' said Hadji Murad, handing Eldar the
gold pieces he had received that day.

Eldar took the money and, going into the light, at once got a
knife from beneath his dagger and began cutting open the
lining of the jacket. Gamzalo half rose and sat with crossed
legs.

'Gamzalo, tell the men to check their guns and pistols and prepare some cartridges. Tomorrow we shall travel far,' said Hadji Murad.

'There is powder and bullets. All will be ready,' said Gamzalo and he growled some incomprehensible remark.

Gamzalo knew why Hadji Murad was ordering them to get their guns loaded. Right from the start he had had only one desire, which as time went on had grown ever stronger: to kill and cut down as many of the Russian dogs as he could and escape to the mountains. He now saw that Hadji Murad wanted this, too, and he was content.

When Hadji Murad had gone, Gamzalo roused his companions and all four spent the night looking over their rifles and pistols, checking the touch-holes and flints, replacing poor ones, priming the pans with fresh powder, filling their cartridge pockets with measured charges of powder and bullets wrapped in oiled rags, sharpening their swords and daggers and greasing the blades with lard.

Near daybreak Hadji Murad again went into the hall to fetch water to wash before praying. The singing of the nightingales as they greeted the dawn was louder and more sustained than in the night. From the nukers' room came the even sound of steel grating and shrilling on stone as a dagger was sharpened. Hadji Murad ladled some water from the tub and had reached his own door when he heard another sound coming from the murids' room besides that of sharpening: it was the thin voice of Khanefi singing a song Hadji Murad knew. Hadji Murad stopped and listened.

Hadji Murad

The song told how the djigit Hamzad and his men drove off a herd of white horses from the Russian side, and how later across the Terck the Russian prince came on him and surrounded him with a great army as thick as a forest. The song wont on to tell how Hamzad slaughtered the horses and with his men held fast behind this bloody rampart of dead horses and fought the Russians as long as there were bullets in their guns and daggers at their belts and blood still flowed in their veins. But before dying Hamzad saw some birds in the sky and cried out to them: ' You birds of the air, fly to our homes and tell our sisters, our mothers and fair maidens that we died for the Ghazalwat. Tell them our bodies shall lie in no grave, our bones will be carried off and gnawed by ravening wolves and black crows will pick out our eyes.'

With these words, sung to a doleful refrain, the song ended, to be followed at once by the cheerful voice of the merry Khan-Mahoma who, as the song finished, bawled 'La itaha illa allay and let out a piercing yell. Then all was quiet and again the only sound was the billing and singing of the nightingales in the garden and, through the door, the even grating and occasional shrilling note of steel slipping rapidly over stone.

Hadji Murad was so lost in thought that he did not notice he was tipping the jug and spilling water over himself. He shook his head reprovingly and went into his room.

When he had finished his morning prayers, Hadji Murad checked his weapons and sat on his bed. There was nothing else to do. To ride out he had to ask permission from the commissioner. It was still dark outside and the commissioner was still asleep.

Khanefi's song reminded Hadji Murad of another song, which his mother had made up. It was about an actual event something that had happened just after he was born, but which he had heard from his mother.

The song was this:

'Your damask blade slashed open my white breast, but I pressed to it my darling boy, and washed him in my hot blood, and the wound healed without help of herbs and roots. I did not fear death, no more will my boy-djigit.'

The words of the song were addressed to Hadji Murad's father. The point of it was that when Hadji Murad was born the khanoum also gave birth to a son (Umma-Khan, her second son) and sent for Hadji Murad's mother to be his wet-nurse as she had been for the khanoum's elder son Abununtsal. But Patimat had not wanted to leave her son and refused to go. Hadji Murad's father got angry and ordered her to. when she still refused he stabbed her with his dagger and would have killed her if she had not been taken away. So, after all, she did not give up her son but raised him, and made up this song about what had happened.

Hadji Murad remembered his mother singing it to him as she put him to bed alongside her, under the fur top-coat on the roof of their house, and he asked her to show him her side where the scar was. He could see his mother just as she was not all wrinkled and grey with missing teeth as when he left her now, but young and beautiful and strong, so strong that even when he was five or six and heavy she carried him in a basket on her back to see his grandfather over the mountains.

And he remembered his grandfather with his wrinkled face and small grey beard. He was a silversmith and Hadji Murad remembered him engraving the silver with his sinewy hands and making him say his prayers. He remembered the fountain at the bottom of the hill where he went with his mother to fetch water, holding on to her trousers. He remembered the skinny dog that used to lick his face, and especially the smell and taste of smoke and sour milk when he followed his mother into the barn where she milked the cow and warmed the milk. He remembered the first time his mother shaved his head and how surprised he had been to see his little round head all blue in the shining copper basin that hung on the wall.

And remembering his childhood, he remembered too his own beloved son Yusuf, whose head he himself had shaved for the first time. Now Yusuf was a handsome young djigit. He remembered him as he last saw him. It was on the day he left Tselmes. His son brought his horse for him and asked if he could ride out and see him off. He was ready dressed and armed and holding his own horse by the bridle. Yusuf's young, ruddy, handsome face and everything about his tall slender figure (he was taller than his father) had seemed the very expression of youthful courage and the joy of living. His shoulders, broad for one so young, his very wide youthful hips and long slender body, his long powerful arms, and the strength, suppleness and dexterity of all his movements were a constant joy to his father and Hadji Murad always regarded his son with admiration.

'You had better stay,' Hadji Murad had said. 'You are the only one at home now. Take care of your mother and grandmother.'

185

And Hadji Murad remembered the look of youthful spirit and pride with which Yusuf, pleased and blushing, had replied that. as long as he lived, no one would harm his mother or grandmother. Yusuf had then, after all, mounted and gone with his father as far as the stream. There he turned back, and since that time Hadji Murad had not seen his wife, mother or son.

And this was the son whose eyes Shamil was going to put out. Of what would happen to his wife he preferred not to think.

Hadji Murad was so agitated by these thoughts that he could not sit still any longer. He jumped up and limped quickly to the door. He opened it and called Eldar. The sun was not yet up, but it was fully light. The nightingales still sang.

'Go and tell the commissioner I want to go riding, and get the horses saddled,' he said.

Butler's only consolation at this time was the romance of military life, to which he surrendered himself not only when on duty but also in his private life. Dressed in Circassian costume, he performed the riding tricks of the natives and with Bogdanovich had twice gone out and lain in ambush, though on neither occasion did they catch or kill anyone. These daring deeds and friendship with Bogdanovich, who was well known for his bravery, seemed to Butler a pleasant and important part of life. He had paid his debt by borrowing the money from a Jew at an enormous rate of interest — which meant that he had simply deferred settling his still unresolved situation. He tried not to think about his situation and, as well as in military romancing, he also sought oblivion in wine. He was drinking more and more heavily and every day advanced his moral decay. He was no longer the handsome Joseph where Marya

Dmitrievna was concerned, on the contrary he made coarse
advances to her, and, much to his surprise, had received a
resolute rebuff which put him thoroughly to shame.

At the end of April a column arrived at the fort under orders
from Baryatinsky to make a new advance through all those
parts of Chechnia which were considered impassable. There
were two companies of the Kabarda Regiment and, according
to established custom in the Caucasus, they were received as
the guests of the units stationed at Kurinskoe. The soldiers
were taken offto the different barracks and were not only given
supper of beef and millet porridge but also served with vodka.
The officers took up quarters with the local officers, who, as
was customary, entertained their visitors.

The party ended with drinking and singing. Ivan Matveevich,
who was very drunk and no longer red, but pale and grey in the
face, sat astride a chair cutting down imaginary enemies with
his drawn sword; he was swearing, laughing, embracing people
and dancing to his favourite song ' In years gone by Shamil
rose up, Ho-ro-ro, Shamil rose up'.

Butler was also present. In this, too, he tried to see the romance
of military life, but deep down he felt sorry for Ivan
Matveevich, though there was no way of stopping him. And
Butler, feeling slightly drunk, quietly left and set off home.

A full moon was shining on the white houses and on the stones
in the road. It was so light you could see every small stone,
every piece of straw and dung on the road. As he approached
thc house Butler met Marya Dmitrievna wearing a shawl over
her head and shoulders. After the rebuff she had given him
Butler had rather shamefacedly avoided her. But now in the

moonlight and under the influence of the wine he had drunk Butler was glad to meet her and tried again to make up to her.

'Where are you going?' he asked.

'To see what the old man is up to,' she answered amicably. She had been quite sincere and positive in her rejection of Butler's advances, but she was displeased that he had been avoiding her of late.

'What's the point of going after him? He'll get home.'

'But will he?'

'If he can't, they'll carry him.'

'That's just it, and it really isn't good enough,' said Marya Dmitrievna. ' You think I shouldn't go then?'

'No, I shouldn't. We had best go home.'

Marya Dmitrievna turned back and began walking to the house with Butler. The moon was so bright that around their shadows moving along the roadside was a moving halo of light. Butler watched this halo round his head and wanted to tell Marya Dmitrievna hat he found her as attractive as ever, but did not know how to begin. She waited for him to speak. Walking thus in silence they had almost reached the house when round the corner appeared some horsemen. It was an officer and escort.

'Who on earth is that?' said Marya Dmitrievna, stepping to the side. The moon was behind the officer and it was only when he was practically level with them that Marya Dmitrievna saw who it was. The officer was Kamenev, who served at one time with Ivan Matveevich and so was known to Marya Dmitrievna.

Peter Nikolaevich,' she said. 'Is that you?'

'In person,' said Kamenev. 'Ah, Butler! How are things? Not asleep yet? Walking out with Marya Dmitrievna, are you? You look out or you'll catch it from Ivan Matveevich. Where is he?'

'You can hear him,' said Marya Dmitrievna, pointing to where there was the sound of singing and a bass drum. 'They're having a binge.'

'Your chaps, is it?'

'No. A column is in from Khasav-Yurt and they're giving them a party.'

'Ah, a good thing. I'll get to it myself. I only want to see him for a minute.

'Is something up?' asked Butler.

'Just a small matter.'

'Good or bad?'

'Depends who for. It's good for us, but tough on others.' And Kamenev laughed.

The couple walking and Kamenev had meanwhile reached Ivan Matveevich's house.

Leo Tolstoy

Kamenev called one of the Cossacks:

'Chikhirev! Here!'

A Don Cossack moved forward from the rest and came up to them. He was in the ordinary Don Cossack uniform, wearing knee-boots and greatcoat, and had saddle-bags slung at the back of his saddle.

'Get it out,' said Kamenev, dismounting.

The Cossack also got off his horse and from one of the saddle-bags drew out a sack with something in it. Kamenev took the sack from the Cossack and put his hand in it.

'Shall I show you the latest, then? You won't be frightened?' he said, turning to Marya Dmitrievna.

'What is there to be afraid of?' said Marya Dmitrievna.

'There you are then,' said Kamenev and he pulled out a man's head and held it up in the moonlight. ' Do you recognize him?'

It was a shaven head, with prominent bulges of the skull over the eyes, trimmed black beard and clipped mustache; one eye was open, the other half-closed; the shaven skull was split and hacked about and the nose covered with black clotted blood. The neck was wrapped in a bloody towel. Despite all the wounds on the head, there was in the set of the now blue lips a childish, good-natured expression.

Marya Dmitrievna took one look and without a word turned and went quickly into the house.

Hadji Murad

Butler could not take his eyes off the terrible head. It was the head of that same Hadji Murad with whom he had recently spent his evenings having such friendly chats.

'How did it happen? Who killed him? Where?' he asked.

'He tried to make a break for it and they caught him,' said Kamenev, and handing the head back to the Cossack he went into the house with Butler.

'He died like a real man,' said Kamenev.

'But how did it all happen?'

'Hang on a minute. When Ivan Matveevich comes I'll give you all the details. That's what I've been sent for. I have got to go round all the forts and villages showing them.'

Ivan Matveevich had been sent for and came back to the house drunk, with two other officers also much the worse for drink, and began embracing Kamenev.

'I have come to see you,' said Kamenev. ' I have brought you the head of Hadji Murad.'

'Go on with you! Has he been killed?'

'Yes, he tried to escape.'

'I always said he would do us down. Where is it then? His lead — let's see it.'

The Cossack was called and came in with the sack containing the head. The head was taken out, and for a long time Ivan Matveevich gazed at it with his drunken eyes.

'He was a fine fellow just the same,' he said. 'Let me kiss him.'

'He was a daredevil chap, that's a fact,' said one of the officers.

When they had all inspected the head they gave it back to the Cossack. The Cossack replaced it in the sack, dropping it carefully so as not to bump it too hard on the floor.

'What do you do, Kamenev — do you say something when you show it round?' asked one of the officers.

'But I want to kiss him,' shouted Ivan Matveevich. ' He gave me a sword.'

Butler went out on to the porch. Marya Dmitrievna was sitting on the second step. she looked round at Butler and at once turned angrily away.

'What's the matter, Marya Dmitrievna?' Butler asked.

'You are just a lot of butchers. You make me sick. Butchers, that's what you are.'

'It can happen to anyone,' said Butler, not knowing what to say. 'That's war.'

'War!' cried Marya Dmitrievna. 'What's war? You are butchers, and that's all there is to it. A dead body should be decently buried and they make mock of it. Butchers, that's what you are!' she repeated and went down the steps and into the house by the back door.

Butler went back to the parlor and asked Kamenev to tell hint in detail what had happened.

And Kamenev told him.

It happened like this.

Hadji Murad was allowed to go riding in the neighborhood of the town provided that he went with a Cossack escort. There was only one troop of Cossacks altogether in Nukha; of these a dozen were detailed for staff duties and if, according to orders, escorts of ten men were sent out it meant that the remaining Cossacks had to do duty every other day. Because of this, after the first day when ten Cossacks were duly sent out, they decided to send only five men, at the same time requesting Hadji Murad not to take his whole party of nukers. However on 25 April all five of them accompanied Hadji Murad when he set off for his ride. As Hadji Murad was mounting, the commandant noticed that all five nukers were preparing to go and told Hadji Murad that he could not take then1 all, but Hadji Murad, appearing not to hear, spurred his horse, and the commandant did not insist. One of the Cossacks was a corporal, Nazarov, who had the St George's Cross, a young, healthy, fresh-faced fellow with light-brown hair cut in a fringe. He was the oldest child of a poor family of Old Believers; he had grown up with no father and kept his old mother, three sisters and two brothers.

193

'See he doesn't go too far, Nazarov,' shouted the commandant.

'Very good, sir,' replied Nazarov. Then, rising on his stirrups and steadying the rifle across his back, he set off at a trot on his big, trusty, long-muzzled chestnut stallion. The other four Cossacks followed him: Ferapontov, who was lean and lanky, the troop's leading pilferer and fixer — he it was who had sold powder to Gamzalo; Ignatov, who was middle-aged and nearing the end of his service, a healthy peasant type who boasted how strong he was; Mishkin, just a weedy boy, too young for active service, of whom everyone made fun; and Petrakov, young and fair-haired, his mother's only son, who was always amiable and cheerful.

It was misty first thing but by breakfast — time it was bright and fine with the sun shining on the freshly burst leaves, the young virginal grass, the shooting corn and the swift, rippling river on the left of the road.

Hadji Murad rode at a walk. The Cossacks and his nukers followed, keeping pace with him. Thus they rode out along the road behind the fort. On their way they met women carrying baskets on their heads, soldiers on wagons and creaking carts drawn by oxen. When they had gone a couple of miles Hadji Murad spurred his white Kabarda horse to a fast amble, and his nukers went into a quick trot. The Cossacks did the same.

'Ay, that's a good horse he's got,' said Ferapontov. 'I'd have him off it, if he was still a hostile like he used to be.'

'Yes, mate, 300 rubles they offered for that horse in Tiflis.'

Hadji Murad

'But I'd beat him on mine,' said Nazarov.

'That's what you think!' said Ferapontov.

Hadji Murad continued to increase the pace.

'Hi there, kunak, you mustn't do that! Not so fast!' shouted
Nazarov, going after Hadji Murad.

Hadji Murad looked back. He said nothing and went on
without slackening pace.

'Watch out, those devils are up to something,' said Ignatov.
'Look how they're going!'

They rode like this towards the mountains for half a mile or so.

'Not so fast, I'm telling you,' Nazarov shouted again.

Hadji Murad did not answer or look back. He simply went
faster and put his horse into a gallop.

'Don't think you'll get away,' shouted Nazarov, stung by this.

He gave his big chestnut stallion the whip and, standing on the
stirrups and leaning forward, rode flat out after Hadji Murad.

The sky was so clear, the air so fresh, Nazarov felt so full of
the joy of life as he flew along the road after Hadji Murad,
merging into one with his powerful, trusty horse that the
possibility of anything wrong or sad or terrible happening
never even occurred to him. He was delighted that with every
stride he was gaining on Hadji Murad and getting close to him.

Leo Tolstoy

Hearing the hoofbeats of the Cossack's big horse getting nearer Hadji Murad realized that he would very soon catch up with him and, seizing his pistol with his right hand, used his left to steady his excited Kabarda which could hear the beat of hoofs behind.

'Not so fast, I say,' shouted Nazarov, now almost level with Hadji Murad and reaching out to seize the bridle of his horse. But before he could catch hold of it a shot rang out.

'What's going on?' cried Nazarov, grasping at his heart. 'Get them, lads!' he said as he swayed and fell forward over the saddle-bow.

But the mountaineers were quicker with their weapons than the Cossacks and fell on them with pistols firing and swords swinging Nazarov hung on the neck of his terrified horse which carried him in circles round his comrades. Ignatov's horse fell and crushed his leg. Two of the mountaineers drew their swords and without dismounting hacked him across the head and arms. Petrakov dashed to his aid but before he could reach him was struck by two bullets, one in the back and one in the side, and he toppled from his horse like a sack.

Mishkin turned his horse back and galloped for the fort. Khanefi and Khan-Mahoma chased after him, but he had too good a start and the mountaineers could not overtake him.

Seeing they could not catch up with him Khanefi and Khan Mahoma returned to their companions. Gamzalo dispatched Ignatov with his dagger and pulled Nazarov down from his horse before slitting his throat too. Khan-Mahoma took off the dead men's cartridge pouches. Khanefi was going to take

Nazarov's horse, but Hadji Murad shouted to him to leave it
and set off down the road. His murids galloped after him,
trying to drive off the horse of Petrakov which followed them.
They were already in the rice-fields two or three miles from
Nukha when the alarm was sounded by a gunshot from the
tower.

Petrakov lay on his back with his stomach slit open, his young
face turned to the sky, gasping like a fish as he lay dying.

'Merciful heavens above, what have they done!' cried the
commander of the fort, clasping his head as he listened to
Mishkin's report and heard of Hadji Murad's escape. 'They've
done for me! Letting him get away — the villains!'

A general alarm was raised. Every available Cossack was sent
off in pursuit of the fugitives, and all the militia from the
peaceable villages who could be mustered were called in as
well. A thousand-ruble reward was offered to anyone bringing
in Hadji Murad dead or alive. And two hours after Hadji Murad
and his companions had ridden away from the Cossacks more
than two hundred mounted men were galloping after the
commissioner to seek out and capture the fugitives.

After traveling a few miles along the main road Hadji Murad
pulled in his panting white horse, which was grey with sweat,
and stopped. Off the road to the right were the houses and
minaret of the village of Belardzhik, to the left were fields, on
the far side of which was a river. Although the way to the
mountains lay to the right Hadji Murad turned left in the
opposite direction, reckoning that pursuers would be sure to
head after him to the right. He meanwhile would make his way
cross-country over the Alazan and pick up the highway again

197

where no one expected him, take the road as far as the forest, then recrossing the river go on through the forest to the mountains. Having made this decision, he turned to the left. But it proved impossible to reach the river. The rice-field which they had to cross had just been flooded, as happened every spring, and it was now a quagmire in which the horses sank up to their fetlocks. Hadji Murad and his nukers turned right and left, expecting to find a drier part, but the field they had struck on was evenly flooded and sodden all over. The horses dragged their feet from the sticky mud with a sound like popping corks and every few paces stopped, panting heavily.

They struggled on like this for so long that when dusk fell they had still not reached the river. To the left was a small island with bushes in first leaf, and Hadji Murad decided to ride into the bushes and stay there till night, resting their exhausted horses.

When they were in the bushes Hadji Murad and his nukers dismounted, hobbled their horses and left them to graze. They themselves ate some of the bread and cheese they had brought with them. The new moon that had been shining sank behind the mountains and the night was dark. There was an unusual abundance of nightingales in Nukha; there were also two in these bushes. In the disturbance caused by Hadji Murad and his men as they rode into the bushes the nightingales fell silent, but as the human noises ceased the birds once more burst into song, calling and answering each other. Hadji Murad, straining his ears to the sounds of the night, listened involuntarily.

The singing of the nightingales reminded him of the song of Hamzad which he had heard the previous night when he went to get the water. Any time now he could find himself in the

198

same situation as Hamzad. It struck him that it would indeed end like that and his mood suddenly became serious! He spread out his cloak and said his prayers. He had scarcely finished when sounds were heard coming towards the bushes. It was the sound of a large number of horses' feet trampling through the quagmire. The keen-eyed Khan-Mahoma ran to one edge of the bushes and in the darkness picked out the black shadows of men on foot and on horseback approaching the bushes. Khanefi saw another large group on the other side. It was Karganov, the district commandant, with his militia. We'll fight them as Hamzad did, thought Hadji Murad.

After the alarm was sounded Karganov had set off in hot pursuit of Hadji Murad with a squadron of militia and Cossacks, but he could find no sign of him or his tracks anywhere. Karganov had given up hope and was on his way back when towards evening they came upon an old Tatar. Karganov asked the old man if he had seen six horsemen. The old Tatar said he had. He had seen six horsemen riding to and fro across the rice-field and then go into the bushes where he collected firewood. Taking the old man with him, Karganov had gone back along the road and, seeing the hobbled horses, knew for certain that Hadji Murad was there. So in the night he had the bushes surrounded and waited till morning to take Hadji Murad dead or alive.

Realizing that he was surrounded, Hadji Murad discovered an old ditch in the middle of the bushes where he decided to make his stand and fight as long as he had ammunition and strength to do so. He told his comrades and ordered them to raise a rampart along the ditch. His nukers at once began cutting off branches and digging earth with their daggers to make a bank. Hadji Murad joined in the work with them.

Leo Tolstoy

As soon as it began to get light the commander of the militia squadron rode up close to the bushes and called out:

'Hey there, Hadji Murad! Surrender! You're outnumbered!'

By way of reply there was a puff of smoke from the ditch, the crack of a rifle and a bullet struck the horse of one of the militiamen, which shied and fell After this there was a rattle of fire from the rifles of the militia positioned on the edge of the bushes. Their bullets whistled and hummed, clipping the leaves and branches and landing in the rampart, but none of them hit the men behind. All they hit was Gamzalo's horse which had strayed off. It was wounded in the head but did not fall; snapping its hobble, it crashed through the bushes to the other horses, nestling against them and spilling its blood on the young grass. Hadji Murad and his men only fired when one of the militiamen showed himself and they seldom missed. Three militiamen were wounded and their comrades not only hesitated to charge Hadji Murad and his men, but dropped farther and farther back, firing only random shots at long range.

This went on for over an hour. The sun had risen half-way up the trees and Hadji Murad was just considering whether to mount and attempt a break for the river when the shouts of a fresh large force of men were heard. This was Hadji-Aha of Mekhtuli and his men. There were about 200 of them. At one time Hadji-Aha had been a kunak of Hadji Murad and lived with him in the mountains, but he had then gone over to the Russians. With him was Akhmet-Khan, the son of Hadji Murad's enemy. Hadji-Aha began as Karganov had done by calling on Hadji Murad to surrender, but as on the first occasion Hadji Murad replied with a shot.

'Out swords and at them!' cried Hadji-Aha, snatching his own from its sheath, and there was a sound of hundreds of voices as men charged shrieking into the bushes.

The militiamen got among the bushes, but several shots in succession came cracking from the rampart. Three or four men fell and the attackers halted. They now opened fire from the edge of the bushes too. They fired and, running from bush to bush, gradually edged towards the rampart. Some managed to get across, while others fell to the bullets of Hadji Murad and his men. Hadji Murad never missed; Gamzalo's aim was no less sure and he gave a delighted yelp each time he saw his bullet strike home. Kurban sat by the edge of the ditch chanting 'La ilaha illa allah'; he took his time in firing, but rarely got a hit. Meanwhile, Eldar was quivering all over in his impatience to rush the enemy with his dagger; he fired often and at random, continually looking round at Hadji Murad and showing himself above the rampart. The shaggy-haired Khanefi continued his role as servant even here. With rolled up sleeves he reloaded the guns as they were handed to him by Hadji Murad and Kurban, carefully ramming home the bullets in oiled rags with an iron ram-rod and priming the pans with dry powder from a horn. Khan-Mahoma did not keep to the ditch like the others, but kept running across to the horses to get them to a safer place, all the time shrieking and casually firing without resting his gun. He was the first to be wounded. He was struck by a bullet in the neck and collapsed backwards spitting blood and cursing. Hadji Murad was wounded next. A bullet went through his shoulder. He tore some wadding from his jacket to plug the wound and went on firing.

'Let's rush them with our swords,' urged Eldar for the third time. He rose above the rampart ready to charge the enemy, but was instantly struck by a bullet. He staggered and fell backwards across Hadji Murad's leg. Hadji Murad looked at him. His handsome sheep's eyes stared earnestly up at him. His mouth, with its upper lip pouting like a child's, quivered but did not open. Hadji Murad freed his leg and went on taking aim. Khanefi bent over Eldar's dead body and quickly began taking the unused cartridges from his cherkeska. Meanwhile Kurban want on chanting, slowly loading and taking aim.

The enemy, whooping and screeching as they ran from bush to bush, were getting nearer and nearer. Hadji Murad was hit by another bullet in the left side. He lay down in the ditch and plugged the wound with another piece of wadding from his jacket. This wound in his side was mortal and he felt that he was dying. One after another images and memories flashed through his mind. Now he saw the mighty Abununtsal Khan clasping to his face his severed, hanging cheek and rush ing at his enemies with dagger drawn; he saw Vorontsov, old, feeble and pale with his sly, white face and heard his soft voice; he saw his son Yusuf, Sofiat his wife, and the pale face, red beard and screwed up eyes of his enemy Shamil.

And these memories running through his mind evoked no feelings in him, no pity, ill-will or desire of any kind. It all seemed so insignificant compared to what was now beginning and had already begun for him. But his powerful body meanwhile continued what it had started to do. Summoning the last remnants of his strength, he lifted himself above the rampart and fired his pistol at a man running towards him. He hit him and the man fell. Then he crawled completely out of the ditch and, with his dagger drawn and limping badly, went straight at the enemy. Several shots rang out. He staggered and fell. A number of militiamen rushed with a triumphant yell towards his fallen body. But what they supposed was a dead body suddenly stirred. First his bloodstained, shaven head, its papakha gone, then his body lifted; then, holding on to a tree, Hadji Murad pulled himself fully up. He looked so terrifying that the advancing men stopped dead. But suddenly he gave a shudder, staggered from the tree, and like a scythed thistle fell full length on his face and moved no more.

He did not move, but could still feel, and when Hadji-Aha, the first to reach him, struck him across the head with his great dagger, he felt he was being hit on the head with a hammer and failed to understand who was doing this and why. This was the last conscious link with his body. He felt no more, and the object that was trampled and slashed by his enemies had no longer any connection with him. Hadji-Alla put a foot on the body's back, with two strokes hacked off its head and rolled it carefully away with his foot so as not to get blood on his boots. Blood gushed over the grass, scarlet from the neck arteries, black from the head.

Karganov, Hadji-Aha, Aklmlet-Khan and the militiamen gathered over the bodies of Hadji Murad and his men (Khanefi, Kurban and Gamzalo were bound) like hunters over a dead beast, standing among the bushes in the gunsmoke, gaily chatting and celebrating their victory.

The nightingales, which were silent while the shooting lasted, again burst into Song, first one near by, then others in the distance.

This was the death that was brought to my mind by the crushed thistle in the ploughed field.

Printed in the United States
105303LV00002B/55-57/A